JOYRIDE

JOYRIDE

GRETCHEN OLSON

BOYDS MILLS PRESS

Copyright © 1998 by Gretchen Olson
Jacket Illustration Copyright © 1998 by Boyds Mills Press
All rights reserved

Published by Caroline House
Boyds Mills Press, Inc.
A Highlights Company
815 Church Street
Honesdale, Pennsylvania 18431
Printed in the United States of America

Publisher Cataloging-in-Publication Data
Olson, Gretchen
  Joyride / by Gretchen Olson — 1st.ed.
[168]p. : ill. ; cm.
Summary: Instead of playing tennis, 17-year-old Jeff is required
to spend his summer working on an Oregon strawberry farm
where new friendships with field hands and migrant workers,
as well as the farmer's daughter, change his outlook.
ISBN 1-56397-758-3
1. Teenagers—Fiction—Juvenile literature. 2. Friendship—
Fiction—Juvenile literature. 3. Farm life—Oregon—Fiction—
Juvenile literature. [1. Teenagers—Fiction. 2. Friendship—
Fiction. 3. Farm life—Oregon—Fiction.] I. Title.
813. 54-dc21 [F] 1998 AC CIP
Library of Congress Catalog Card Number: 97-70580

First Boyds Mills Press paperback Edition, 1999
Book designed by Tim Gillner
The text of this book is set in 11-point Berkeley book.

10 9 8 7 6 5 4 3 2 1

For Ginny, Julia, and Phil,
with love

Also for Macario, José Luis, Bertoldo, Gilberto,
Loreto, Matias, Miguel, Pablo, and Tomás.

Acknowledgements

Special thanks to Ellen Howard for "exceedingly close."

To my critique group for endless support and encouragement: Sharon Thompson, Cindy Wall, Mary Finnegan, Sandra Mages.

To Sharon Michaud, my kindred spirit scribe, and Kathy Beckwith, who shares a passion for this craft.

Thanks to Linda Crew for patiently answering so many questions.

I am also grateful for the technical advice I received from Steve Catlett, manager, Carriage House Fruit; Carolyn Chapin, Spanish teacher; Juana González-Chavez, ESL instructor; Craig Koessler, head tennis pro, Illahe Hills Country Club; Sgt. Tracie Domogalla, Yamhill County Sheriff's Office; Dr. Eduardo González-Viaña, for "walking through sky;" and Mary Lou Polvi, swimmer mom.

Chapter 1

JEFF MCKENZIE UNTIED HIS SHOES and wondered if he'd ever play tennis again.

He kicked them onto the hard ground and winced as a sharp twig poked through his sock. What a crummy place to change. The oak knoll was littered with dried leaves, fallen branches, dead weeds, and little brown puffballs. But he wasn't about to change clothes at school. The guys had razzed him enough already. "Goin' to work with the beaners, Kenzie?" "How do ya want your tortillas? Rare or well-done?" Then they'd laughed and punched him in the arm and slapped his back.

Now the shade of the tall trees brought a quick chill to his legs as he took off his pants; his thigh muscles tightened. He yanked a navy blue T-shirt over his head and tossed it to the ground. The graphics and letters scrunched together, but he knew the words: *Madrona Hills Fourth of July Invitational*. He grimaced. Slim chance he'd be there this year—he'd be lucky to even practice in the next three weeks.

He shoved his legs into a pair of Levi's and pulled on a

long-sleeved denim work shirt. As he began buttoning, his eyes followed a twisted oak limb reaching high into a dense, leafy canopy. He stared and the leaves blurred. The reluctant thought drifted back again . . . he wished he hadn't helped Paul celebrate.

One thing had led to another that night. Soon he and Paul were driving out west of Salem and then down some county back road, Jeff's Bronco II zigging and zagging and skidding on the gravel. It was awesome—until the field. That big, open field, calling to them.

Why not? Windows rolled down, music turned up. It felt great bumping across the rows, swirling in tight turns, digging into the dirt. Great. Until they hit something.

"Jake Hampton's the name," the farmer had said later that night as Jeff's parents stood on the front porch in their bathrobes. "Shall we settle this ourselves? Or shall I call the police?"

Jeff had rolled his eyes. Just what he needed—flashing lights announcing to the neighborhood that such-a-nice-boy Jeffery Taylor McKenzie had turned into a rotten vandal.

Jeff's father cleared his throat. "We can take care of it."

"I'd like to see them work it off." The farmer nodded at Jeff and Paul.

Paul shuffled his feet and caught Jeff's eye.

"Oh, yeah," said Jeff, "uh, my buddy, here, didn't have anything to do with this. It was my idea."

His father looked over his glasses.

"It was all my idea." Jeff crossed his arms. "He tried to stop me."

"Well, then, young man," said Mr. Hampton, his broad hands on his hips, "in order to replace that irrigation motor, it'll mean three to four week's work for you."

"But Jeffery has tennis practice and tournaments," said his mother, stepping to the edge of the porch.

Mr. Hampton stared at her. "Excuse me, ma'am, but starting in a week, I've got forty acres of strawberries to harvest, and perishable crops do not wait for tennis tournaments."

She was about to speak again when Mr. McKenzie grasped her shoulder. "He'll do it." Jeff's father glanced around the group, then at Jeff. "He'll be there—and he'll do the job."

Now, wishing it had all been a bad dream, Jeff bent for a boot, crammed in his foot, and pulled out the tongue. He jerked the leather laces through the metal holes, around the hooks, and into a double knot. Three or four weeks away from the courts, he lamented, grabbing the other boot. What a waste. He'd lose his rhythm, his speed—his ranking.

He walked from the shade of the oaks into the bright June sunlight and closed his eyes for a moment. What a way to celebrate the last day of school. Everyone else had gone to BJ's and then to the courts or the club pool. Everyone else was going to have an incredible summer.

"You'll be working with my two daughters and my wife," Mr. Hampton had told Jeff, "running the picking crew, weighing flats, loading trucks."

Wonderful, he thought, retracing his path through the wild grass and thistles. Me and the womenfolk, down on the farm. He climbed over the sagging barbed wire fence and walked in front of his Bronco, ignoring the dented frame.

The gravel road seemed wider now as he drove in a straight line. It dipped and climbed, a low ridge forming on the right and a valley on the left. Green and brown fields spread across the broad valley floor, patched together with bushy fence rows, dotted with old barns, farmhouses, clumps of trees, and an occasional pond.

As the road eased downhill, Jeff spotted a white house next to a lake. A barn stood behind the house and three long buildings lined the far side. According to Mr. Hampton's brief directions, the strawberries were past the grain tanks. "Don't worry," he'd said, "you'll see the cars."

There they were. Pickups, vans, cars, bumper-to-bumper, hugging the ditch. A woman leaned against a gray van. She held a small child in diapers. Two other children peered out the rear door, their dark eyes studying him.

He found a vacant spot, parked, and locked his car. Pausing, he took in the field stretched out before him. Row after row of thick, lush foliage marched in straight lines to the lake. A dirt road cut through the middle and another road crossed precisely at center, creating four equal sections. Tall stacks of yellow containers and two blue outhouses stood along the crossroad.

"NO CARS IN THE FIELD." The sign posted at the field entrance was in English and Spanish. Jeff sucked in a deep breath, let it out slowly, and began walking down the hard dirt drive. Pickers heading to their cars carried buckets, jackets, and grocery sacks. Their shirts hung loose and their pants drug about their tennis shoes. Mud and berry stains padded their knees.

Jeff avoided eye contact. Maybe they'd think he was staring. Maybe they'd say something he wouldn't understand.

They passed him in silence, then broke into chatter and laughter, a sure sign, he figured, they were talking about him and his new *gringo* clothes.

A handful of pickers still crouched over the dark green rows. Others stood in a line at the crossroads, their arms cradling yellow boxes filled with strawberries. Their eyes focused on a girl weighing the boxes and punching white cards. As she punched, a worker whisked the crates to a nearby truck.

"You made it," Mr. Hampton called to Jeff from the rear of the truckbed. "We can use you. Bring over those flats from Alexa's scale."

Here we go, Jeff thought grimly. Farm work at its best. He moved to the scale as a picker set two containers on the metal platform. Alexa shook her head and studied his ticket. "Lorenzo Perez. *Muchas fresas*. Forty-one pounds. Too much. The berries get smashed. *No mucho*, okay?"

"*Sí, no mucho*." He grinned, gave several quick nods, and stuffed his ticket inside his baseball cap.

Alexa sighed and grabbed the flats.

"I'll get 'em." Jeff stopped her.

She stared.

"I'm Jeff—Jeff McKenzie."

Her eyes narrowed. "The one who tore up my bean field?" The corner of her mouth pulled tight.

Jeff swallowed.

She stepped aside.

He reached for the flats. The weight tugged at his arms, and the plastic rims dug into his fingers. God, he panicked, what if I drop these? He held his breath, turned, stepped once, twice, three times, then swung them up to the truck.

The flats barely cleared the steel edge, landing with a thud on the wooden surface. Thank you, he thought with relief.

Mr. Hampton was gone. Now the man who'd been helping Alexa stood on the truck. He snatched up Jeff's flats, swiftly adding them to the load.

"Looks easy, huh?" A girl walked up to the truck holding a single crate.

The man returned and smiled down at her, wrinkles creasing into his dark brown skin. *"Gracias,"* he said, leaning to take her fruit.

The girl was younger and a whole lot friendlier than Alexa. Freckles ran across her nose and cheeks. She studied Jeff. "Are you the one who got in our field?"

He felt his neck heat up. Geezuz. Was everyone going to drill him?

"Why'd you do it?"

For fun, Jeff remembered. Even now he felt the exhilaration as he raced into that endless space. Each move was his, each turn, each circle. And Paul, laughing, yelling. For a brief moment, he'd been out of this world, out of himself. Wrong answer. He cleared his throat. "Uh, I don't know."

How could a few lousy strawberries weigh so much? Don't think about it, he warned. Keep moving. Be ready for the weight. A little slack in the arms. Bend and lift, step to the truck and heave ho. He worked into a rhythm, keeping pace with Alexa, grabbing the flats off her scale before she had a chance to set them on the ground.

The line finally dwindled. Jeff stood behind Alexa while she weighed a woman's single flat.

"¿Muy rojo, sí?" The woman said eagerly.

"Sí, very red," Alexa answered.

"¿Para mí?" She held up a bucket partially filled with berries. Then she pulled a small coin purse from her pants pocket.

"No, it's okay." Alexa punched the lady's ticket. "Just take them."

"Gracias."

Jeff stepped to the scale just as Alexa grasped the flat. She whipped around, whacking it into Jeff's stomach, and losing her grip. Berries poured to the ground. Jeff dropped to one knee and caught the flat. More berries scattered, but Alexa regained a firm hold and Jeff slowly straightened up. They stood for moment, holding the flat between them. Alexa's blond bangs stuck to her sweaty forehead and a berry stain brushed across her cheek. Jeff tried not to smirk. What do you say to someone who doesn't like you but looks so stupid?

"Sorry," Alexa mumbled. She looked at the ground. "Guess I'd better get these."

"Don't you wash them?" Jeff picked up a dirty strawberry.

She shook her head. "This is nothing. We've knocked over entire stacks."

A lady holding a clipboard and wearing a straw hat walked out of a nearby row. "You must be Jeff." Another woman came up behind her with an armful of empty flats. The second one was out of breath. She set the flats next to the scale. "There ya go, Lexie."

"Thanks," said Alexa, walking to the truck.

The clipboard lady extended her hand. "I'm Maggie Hampton."

Jeff shook her hand.

"This is Ethel Gormley, our neighbor and number one row boss."

"Howdee." Ethel pushed her sunglasses on top of her head, took a Coke from a small cooler, and held it against her puffy red cheeks.

Jeff waited. Would these women get their jabs in, too?

"I don't suppose my husband introduced you before he left." Mrs. Hampton pointed to the girls. "Our daughters, Libby and Alexa."

Libby was sitting on a stack of empty flats eating a candy bar. "Hi." Chocolate coated her braces.

"We met," said Alexa flatly, her back to the group.

"And this is Macario Espinoza." Mrs. Hampton nodded to the guy on the truck. "He runs the place."

Macario removed his White Sox baseball cap, ran his hand through his shiny black hair, and readjusted the hat.

"Ethel and I have to check the berries in section two for tomorrow." Mrs. Hampton took a Coke from the cooler. "Macario needs to get to the cannery. And the rest of you need to clean up the field."

"Aw, Mom," said Libby. "It's just the first day."

"We don't want to get behind, sweetie." She handed black plastic garbage bags to Libby, Jeff, and Alexa. "Besides, there could be some real finds out there."

"Right," Libby grumbled, scuffing toward the field.

Alexa followed. "Take a couple rows," she told Jeff, "and get all the junk—wheelies, flats, garbage."

"Wheelies?" Jeff started down the closest aisle and immediately tripped over something. "What the—?"

"Wheelies," answered Alexa, slinging one over her shoulder. "Little wire carts."

"They're regular booby traps." He brushed off his hands.

"You okay?" Libby picked a berry and popped it in her mouth.

"Yeah." Jeff grabbed a muddy jacket left alongside the row.

"There's a 'ost-and-found 'ox." Libby tried to talk and chew at the same time. She wiped her mouth on the sleeve of her Portland Trail Blazer T-shirt while pointing to the scales. Jeff crammed the jacket under his arm.

Something shiny white poked out from under a berry bush. Jeff started for it, then stopped. He nudged it with his foot and his stomach lurched. Some find. He carefully pushed the diaper into his black bag.

Chapter 2

"THE FARMER IN THE DELL, the farmer in the dell, heigh-ho the derry-o . . . "

"Cut it out, Mark," Jeff snapped.

"Did you milk the cows and slop the pigs?"

Jeff glared across the dinner table at his younger brother.

"Okay, boys, that's enough," said his mother. "Have some salad, Jeffery."

Jeff's father passed the glass bowl. "How was your first day?"

"Well—" he started, then stopped. He stared at his plate. "Do I really need to do this farm thing?" Before his father could argue, he went on. "I know I screwed up and I'm sorry, okay? Can't I do something else to pay off this Hampton guy? I could work at the club again, teach a few tennis lessons. Even the Yogurt Palace would be better than this."

"You can have my paper route," said Mark.

"Forget it."

"Herb, maybe we could talk to the club manager," Jeff's mother said to her husband.

"Remember, Suzanne, Jeff got himself into this mess and he can get himself out."

"That's my point," said Jeff. "Let me, for once, solve my own problem."

Jeff's father leaned forward, crossing his arms on the table. "You need to repay Mr. Hampton by working on his farm. It's the appropriate consequence."

Jeff looked at the ceiling and sighed. Then he thought of something. He cleared his throat. "Just how appropriate is it," he said, pausing, "to be completely surrounded by Mexicans?"

His father frowned.

This might work. Jeff knew his father's speeches by heart—about the rising number of Mexicans in the daily police reports, about illegal immigrants on welfare and in the schools and unionizing against farmers.

"It's true," Jeff pushed. "The strawberry fields are crawling with them. They're everywhere. Who knows how safe it is."

"There aren't any Americans?" his father asked.

"Well, yeah, there's the Hamptons, and this row boss lady, Ethel, but that's it." He didn't add the local kids who'd be starting the next morning. "No one else speaks English. It's *sí* this, *sí* that. And the Spanish music." He rolled his eyes. "It's gonna drive me nuts."

His father was silent. Finally, he said, "I don't imagine Mr. Hampton would allow his wife and daughters to work in an unsafe situation."

"The farmer in the dell . . . " Mark started softly.

★   ★   ★

Jeff smacked off the alarm. He winced at the ache in his arms, and buried his head in the pillow. He dared to peek at the clock: 4:02. He groaned.

16

Knowing it wouldn't get any easier, he forced his legs over the side of the bed. Pushing himself up, he lost his balance and bumped against a bookshelf. Something crashed to the floor. He switched on a light and retrieved the brass trophy. "MADRONA HILLS INVITATIONAL, SECOND PLACE, MEN'S SINGLES," read the engraving. He placed it back on the shelf next to a bunch of little plastic ones holding fake gold tennis balls. There were other awards with silver players and bronze rackets, marble bases and shiny plaques.

He glanced at Andre Agassi, frozen in mid-serve on a Nike poster. "I know, I know—just do it. And just *when* do you suggest I do it?"

★　★　★

"Dear Jeffery, Have a nice day. Here's a lunch. Please ask if you can get Saturday off for your Hillsboro tournament. Please pick up Mark from baseball practice tonight. I have a teachers' dinner and Dad has a meeting. Love, Mom." He crumpled the note, grabbed the sack lunch and a piece of cold pizza.

As he stepped outside, cool air tingled against his face. He took in a deep breath and a chill spread through his chest. For a moment he stood listening. There was no sound. Not even the distant bark of a dog. Too quiet, he thought. He started his Bronco and pushed in a CD.

A hundred pickers, Mrs. Hampton had said, now with school out. Geezus, how in the world do you control a hundred people in a berry field? His stomach churned. All he wanted was one opponent on a tennis court. *I won't ever ask for anything else again. I promise.*

As he approached the outskirts of West Salem, subdivisions and sidewalks gave way to long gravel driveways and older homes with separate garages. There were no more traffic signals or street lights, only a few bright mercury-vapor barn lights.

A Pepsi sign flickered outside a little grocery store. Martha's Market. Jeff's stomach grumbled again. Maybe some milk would dilute his breakfast pizza.

A bell jangled as he pushed open the door, and a group of field hands watched as he walked to the cooler. With a quart of milk in one hand and a pint of Pepto-Bismol in the other, Jeff stood silently in line. The lady at the cash register said something in Spanish to the men. Were they talking about him?

He set his remedy on the counter and the lady cocked her head. "Ahh, so, a *vaca rosa*. What's the matter, honey, not feeling well?" Jeff shrugged. He hated being called "honey."

"Listen," she said more gently, "go heavy on the Pepto and you'll feel better. Just leave it to ol' Martha and you'll have a great day." She grabbed a roll of Lifesavers and tossed them in his bag. "You know peppermint—it calms what riles ya." She smiled. One eye looked straight at him but the other one stuck to the inside corner. He wasn't sure which eye to look at.

"Thanks," Jeff answered, not in the mood for early morning cheerfulness. Martha and his mom would get along great. Back in the car he took a few swallows of milk and then downed some Pepto. He pulled out of the parking lot and turned at the blinking yellow light. The empty county road lay before him, cutting between acres and acres of open fields. He passed gnarled orchards, rolling vineyards, and flocks of sheep grazing in thick pastures. Fanning out across the clear, broad western skyline were the soft peaks and tree-lined ridges of the Coast Range.

Leaving pavement, he turned onto the gravel of

Bethel Road. Rocks bounced up against his car. He slowed down. Damn gravel. Stupid job. He almost had his dad convinced, bringing up that stuff about Mexicans on Hampton's farm. But his dad was hard to figure. On the one hand, he would complain that Mexicans took advantage of the American system. Then another day, he'd gripe that Americans wouldn't think of working in the fields, that they'd rather collect unemployment than do stoop labor. Once, when his dad was moaning about Mexicans, Jeff had accused him of being racist.

"I am not," his dad had bristled. "Just look at my dental practice. I've got a number of black and Hispanic patients."

Nice try, but it sounded like he was filling a square: check. Like when he visited his mother once a month in Medford: check. Or made his annual contributions to the Boy Scouts and Oregon Public Broadcasting: check, check.

All Jeff's mom ever saw were the "cute little Mexican children" at her elementary school. "Oh, those big trusting brown eyes and that gorgeous black hair," she'd say. "And they're always so dressed up."

As Jeff passed the grain tanks, he could see a string of cars already parked alongside the strawberry field. Pickers stood visiting in small groups. Five or six children sat on a blanket near the entrance, eating from a pile of berries. Jeff felt his eyes drawn across the road to a bean field. *The* bean field. His chest tightened. Green, leafy sprouts grew in perfect order down tidy rows. But there, even after a week, were his tire marks, cutting circles and mashing plants into the ground. He unrolled his window. The air smelled of damp grass.

"Hey, Jeff McKenzie!"

Libby straddled a four-wheeler at the entrance to the

strawberry field. She revved the engine and signaled for him to follow. Whipping around, she roared back down the dirt road, her hair bouncing about her ears.

Jeff drove slowly through a shallow ditch. The field was empty and quiet. Row upon row of plants stood ready, their leaves covered with a shiny dew, clumps of red heart-shaped berries hanging heavy against the ground.

He pulled close to the last row and hurried over to the truck. "Sorry I'm late."

"You're okay," said Mrs. Hampton, zipping up her sweatshirt. "We're just about to start."

Ethel sat in her lawn chair, finishing a maple bar and cup of coffee. She wore the same berry-stained jeans she had on the day before. "Mornin'." She wiped her mouth with her hand.

Alexa walked around the truck carrying her scale. She headed straight for a short stack of empty flats and set the scale down. Then she placed two empty flats on the platform and began fussing with a knob.

"Umph," grunted Libby, also carrying a scale from the truck. She lowered it onto another makeshift table and stood up. "Whew." She looked at Jeff and her face brightened. "Hi."

"Hi."

Mrs. Hampton flipped through the papers on her clipboard. "Ethel and I'll be assigning rows and filling out I-9s and W-4s. Jeff, you can help Macario move more flats to the headland. We didn't unload enough empties there last night." She pointed toward the main entrance. The tangled group of pickers had formed a line now and were moving past the mountain of flats, lifting ten or more off in one smooth motion, balancing them on their heads as they scattered out between the rows.

"They're missing some rows," Jeff said.

Ethel grabbed a clipboard. "They pick two at a time."

"Two?"

"Not my idea." She picked something out of her teeth. "It's a pain keeping track of 'em."

Macario appeared from behind the truck, carrying a metal cash box and two empty coffee cans.

"*Gracias.*" Alexa began arranging picker tickets in one can, pens and pencils in another. She took a silver hand-punch from the cash box and gave it to Libby. It dangled from a loop of green yarn. Alexa had an identical one which she immediately slipped over her head.

"Nice necklace," Jeff said, testing Alexa's mood. He had to be here, he figured, so might as well be friendly.

"Valuable necklace," Alexa corrected him, dryly.

"Oh, yeah?" He matched her tone. Why not? If she was going to dish it out, she could darn well take it.

She eyed him. "Each punch has its own design. Mine is a diamond and Libby's is a star." Alexa squeezed the handles.

"And," Libby said, stepping closer, "if someone ever stole 'em, they could add a zillion pounds to their ticket." She madly punched at the air. Then she looked at Jeff and giggled.

Geezuz, now what? Was his fly down?

Alexa pointed to his mouth.

"You've got a pink mustache," Libby told him.

Jeff rubbed his lips. "Gone?"

They both nodded.

"*¿Listo?*" Macario asked Jeff.

Jeff stared blankly.

"You are ready?" Macario pointed to the pickup.

"Oh, sure."

Working together in silence, they quickly had a full

load. They drove the wobbling, empty flats to the field entrance where the faster pickers had already moved forward, leaving occasional gaps in a line of kneeling bodies. Nearby, a young boy was dividing handfuls of gravel between several children. They gleefully snatched the rocks and took turns tossing them at a line scratched in the dirt.

"¡Maco, *mi paisano*!" A man wearing an Oregon Ducks baseball hat stood in a nearby row.

Jeff watched as the two men locked hands, first in a traditional handshake and then, like a well-rehearsed dance step, their hands slipped forward and grasped each other's thumb. Laughing, they embraced.

Macario signalled to Jeff. "This is Antonio Manuel Flores. He is a *paisano*—a friend from home. This is Jeff—" He halted.

"McKenzie."

"*Sí*, Jeff McKenzie. *Él trabaja para el Señor* Hampton this summer."

"*Mucho gusto*," said Antonio. "And this is *mi esposa*—Angélica.

"Nice to meet you," said Jeff to a woman squatting in the next row.

She smiled shyly. "*El gusto es mío.*" Her eyes shone as they darted from Macario to Jeff. Then she bent over the bush, her fingers darting through the foliage, parting the leaves, gathering a handful of berries, then moving to the next section. Both hands were overflowing when she dumped the load into her bucket.

A van and two cars pulled to the side of Bethel Road, and an army of town kids and adults poured out with water jugs, lunch coolers, radios, and an assortment of picking containers—coffee cans, butter tubs, plastic buckets.

More cars came by, dropped kids off, and drove on.

One man climbed out of his car, yelling after his boy, "Listen here, Danny, you do a good job, or else."

"Or else what?" the boy grumbled to his friend as they walked past Jeff.

"We're full right here," Ethel announced, stepping quickly across the berry rows. "I need you all starting in the back." She pointed toward the lake. "Use the flats by the truck."

Stopping in front of Jeff, she handed him the clipboard. "Here, take these folks to the far end of section two. Write down the row number and the person's name. Tell them to pick clean and no stems." She did an about-face and marched away.

Jeff looked at Macario. "Is she in charge around here?"

Macario chuckled. "No. We all do it together."

"Where's Mr. Hampton?"

"He is a very busy *patrón*—making everything to work. He drive around, check on the people, fix broken tractor. But most of time, he is talking to the telephone and the computer."

Macario said goodbye to the couple and then told Jeff, "I unload the pickup and I move pipe in the corn. When you put the flats on the truck, just twenty high, *¿sí?*"

"Sure—twenty high." Jeff's mind raced, but there was no time to think. Already the new pickers were wandering around section two.

"Don't skip any rows," shouted Alexa as he jogged past the scales.

It was like herding ducks, but finally everyone was squatting or standing beside a row. Jeff checked a wooden stake and jotted down the number. "Hello, sir, may I get your name?"

"Jacobs. Frank Jacobs. How are the berries today?"

How are the berries? What kind of a question was that? They're just fine, thank you, but they wish you wouldn't pick them.

"Are there lots of big ones?"

"Yeah, lots." Jeff shook his head and moved down the rows, writing names, bending to hear muffled voices against the blare of radios.

"Name?" Jeff asked a boy sitting cross-legged in his row.

"What's it to ya?" It was the kid whose dad had yelled at him. Skinny thing with holes in his jeans and a faded brown T-shirt.

Jeff cleared his throat. "I need your name on this form."

The boy looked at his friend and smirked. "Santa Claus."

Jeff looked for help. Ethel and Mrs. Hampton were still in section one, Alexa and Libby were weighing flats, and pickers were now eyeing him.

A berry sailed through the air, hitting a girl on the back.

"Hey, cut it out!" Jeff glared at the skinny kid.

"So fire me."

"So plan on it."

"Sounds good."

"Listen, kid, do you want to work or not?"

"I don't want to pick any stinkin' berries on any stinkin' farm. You can take them and shove 'em up—"

"Okay, here's the deal." Jeff dropped his clipboard to his side and stuck the pencil above his ear. "These aren't my strawberries and I don't give a rip what you do here. You can sit on your rear all day if you want. Just don't bug me."

"Don't freak, man." The kid raised his hands to his chest. Berry slime spread across his palms. "I'll be good."

"Okay, I need a name or you're history."

Words spit into the air: "Danny Stevens."

Chapter 3

A WHISTLE SHRILLED across the berry field. "Lunch!" Ethel hollered. "Weigh your berries or take them with you."

Rising awkwardly, pickers stretched their arms and legs and arched their backs. Kids shuffled to the scales with half-filled flats or ran to the end of their rows, gathering mini-coolers and paper sacks, and headed for the shade of a giant oak tree at the edge of the field. A few workers returned to their cars.

Jeff covered a stack of berry-filled flats with an empty container. He stepped back. Not bad. Standing there, perfectly straight, were twenty-four towers of yellow flats, twenty high. And not a single one out of sync, tilting, or smashing the fruit.

"Good job."

He spun around.

Mrs. Hampton set her clipboard on the end of the truckbed. "Did you bring a lunch?"

"It's in my car."

"You're welcome to join us." She pulled a cooler from

the shady side of the truck. "We stick around the scales—seems like there's always someone who needs to get weighed."

Libby and Alexa were still punching tickets. Ethel lumbered into the circle, wiping her forehead with her shirtsleeve. "Gettin' warm out there." She dragged a lawn chair from behind the stacks of empty flats and flopped it open.

Join the ladies for lunch. Great. Jeff stuffed his hands in his back pockets and gazed out across the berry field to the lake's still waters, then on to the Coast Range. The rolling charcoal peaks fused with the thin, ice-blue sky. Perfect day for tennis. He looked down at his dusty boots. For as long as he could remember, summer meant tennis. First as a little kid with beginner lessons in the mornings, then splashing around in the club pool. The lessons got longer and the pool got deeper. Then came tournaments and exchanges. Locker room parties and late-night swims. Invitationals, sectionals, regionals. Talk of scholarships. Now, with college only a year away, would he be able to keep it up?

"Aren't ya gonna eat?" Libby's head craned backward as she looked up at him. She took a bite of candy bar.

"Maybe."

"You'd better—you'll get hungry."

"You sound like my mother." Jeff jumped to the ground, his leather boots tugging at his feet like lead weights. Walking to the Bronco, he took off his flannel shirt and savored the air slipping around his neck and under his white T-shirt. He opened the driver's door, smelled warm tuna fish, and groaned.

"You can sit with me," offered Libby when he returned. She patted the wooden planks of the flatbed.

He pulled himself up.

"You want a carrot?" She shoved one in his face. Jeff jerked back. "I'll pass."

"Don't be a pest, Libby," said Mrs. Hampton.

"I'm not." She frowned. *Am I?*"

"You're okay," Jeff muttered.

Libby sat up straight, raising her eyebrows to her mom.

Jeff snapped open a pop. What a switch from last summer. He would have just finished teaching a bunch of twelve-year-olds the backhand when Debbie would arrive with a deli picnic from Nordstrom's. They'd relax beneath the maple trees lining the tennis courts, the grass cool against their legs, music from the club drifting across the lawn. Debbie's long, soft hair brushing against his face . . .

Jeff suddenly realized he was staring at Ethel's bottom, straining the nylon folding chair, making it sag close to the ground.

A woman pushed her wheelie up to Alexa's scale and paused, trying to catch her breath.

"I'll get them," said Alexa, moving in front of the scale, bending to lift the top flat. Her tanned, broad shoulders tightened beneath a loose, purple tank top. Her arm muscles firmed. She stood, turned, and set the flat on her scale. She bent again, lifting another flat. "Big berries." Alexa smiled at the woman.

"*Sí, jitomates.*"

"You're right," she said, punching the woman's ticket, "tomatoes."

Jeff watched more closely now as Alexa moved the flats off the scale two at a time. Nice. Really nice build. She could have an awesome tennis serve with those shoulders.

"Lexie, you're getting burned." Mrs. Hampton pulled

a tube of sunscreen from her cooler and tossed it to her. "You too, Libby."

"Then I won't get tanned." Libby held her arm next to Jeff's. "Man, you're really dark. How'd you do that?"

"Lots of court time."

Libby looked puzzled.

"Tennis."

"Mom, I wanna play tennis." Libby wrinkled her forehead. "Is it hard?" she asked Jeff.

"Nothin' to it. Just hit the ball over the net."

"I don't believe it," said Alexa indignantly. She stood at the scale with her back to Jeff.

What the—? His mind tumbled. How could she possibly be mad? He was just kidding around. Besides, what'd she know about tennis? Geezuz, girl, get a life.

"Would ya look at them!" Alexa pointed to the field entrance. "Driving in here like they owned the place. Can't they read?"

Jeff spotted a car slowly working its way along the main road.

"Probably some u-pickers," said Mrs. Hampton casually. She removed her straw hat and tried to cram loose strands of light brown hair into a gold barrette. Standing up, she adjusted the hat. "Well, Ethel, shall we?"

"The afternoon push," groaned Ethel. She began rubbing Coppertone 15 on her ears and face, smearing it into her short, blond-streaked hair.

"You girls won't be busy for a while," said Mrs. Hampton. "I'd like you to take turns checking behind the younger pickers."

"Ah, Mom, we end up picking their dirty rows." Libby slurped the last of her pop. "It's a major pain."

"Are you complaining?"

Libby scowled. "No."

"WNWP836, unit one to unit nine, Maggie." Mr. Hampton's voice filled the air.

Mrs. Hampton unhooked the black handheld radio from her belt. "Unit nine."

"How's it going?"

"We just finished lunch and are heading back out. The berries look good. Still first pick though," she said, glancing at the truck. "We'll only have one load today."

"A crew's coming in the morning to train boysenberry canes," answered Mr. Hampton. "I've gotta run over to Carlton for gloves, then I need to load wheat for Portland. How's that Jeff kid doing?"

Jeff tensed.

"Fine."

"Good. Unit one clear."

"Unit nine clear." Mrs. Hampton returned the radio to her belt and tucked the clipboard under her arm. "Come on, Libby."

Libby released a dramatic sigh, grabbed a bucket from off the ground, and trudged after her mother.

Mrs. Hampton pressed the silver whistle to her lips. A pulsating screech crossed the field. "Let's get goin'!"

"Where do you want the u-picks, Mom?" Alexa called.

"Any of these closer rows. Just make sure they flag it when they're done."

Jeff began loading lunchtime flats onto the truck. "So what's the big deal about u-pickers?" he asked Alexa. "Do they eat more than they pay for?"

"No."

Well, that was an award-winning conversation, thought Jeff. Why do you even try, McKenzie? Just shut up, man, ignore her and load the stupid berries. He hoisted himself onto the flatbed.

"They're annoying," Alexa said, her eyes fixed on the

car approaching the crossroad. "We have that sign at the entrance for a reason, but they totally ignore it. There's no room in the field for extra cars—they end up hitting row markers and smashing plants."

Jeff cringed. Did she emphasize the smashing bit?

Alexa dribbled sunscreen up one arm and began working it in. "It's my mom's idea." She lifted her ponytail and massaged lotion on her neck. "There aren't many places where you can get fresh berries. She figures it's a community service." She finished her other arm as the pale blue Ford Galaxy stopped. A gray-haired man stuck his head out the window. "Is this where you get the berries?"

"Yes." Alexa faked pleasant pretty well.

The man helped his wife from the car. She looked out of place in her flowered dress and shiny shoes, a white purse hanging over her arm. "Do you have Bentons?"

"Not yet," said Alexa, leaning on one hip. "We're in the Totems."

"We wanted the sweeter berries for jam," the lady said.

"Lots of people think Totems are just as sweet. Why don't you try them?"

"Oh, dear. I don't know. Could I buy just a small batch?"

Alexa turned to Jeff. "Is there a 'small batch' in the stack?"

He sorted through the pile and offered a half-filled flat for inspection.

"Those look awfully orange, don't you think, Henry?"

"Don't fuss about it, Lucille. Just take them."

Alexa weighed the flat. "Eight pounds. At sixty cents a pound, that'll be four dollars and eighty cents, plus a two dollar deposit on the container."

A shriek and chorus of laughter rose from the field.

Jeff turned in time to see some kid throw a berry and another kid dive low in the row.

"You guys get picking," Alexa shouted as she eyed the blue Galaxy now maneuvering around the intersection.

"There aren't enough ripe ones." It was the same boy who'd argued with Jeff that morning. Danny something. No wonder he couldn't find the ripe ones—his hair hung in his eyes.

"You've got to finish those rows before you go home."

A chorused whine went up. "We'll never finish."

"You won't standing there. Now get goin'." She pointed at their rows. "They drive me absolutely crazy." Alexa gripped her handpunch. "I forget what lousy pickers kids are."

"Why use them?" asked Jeff.

"Equal opportunity or something. I don't know, it's ridiculous. Dad says we only need three Mexicans per acre."

"That sounds pretty bad." Jeff crossed his arms and leaned against the truck, wondering how she'd respond.

Alexa frowned. "How do you figure? It's a compliment. They're good pickers."

"It sounds racist." Jeff pushed a little further. For some reason, he felt like drawing her into an argument, especially one she might lose.

"Listen," she said, her voice rising, "it takes five American adults or ten American kids to pick the same acre. If you want, I'll give you total pounds at the end of the day and the numbers will speak for themselves. That's hardly racist."

She began walking away, then turned back. "For your information, some of these people are like family. They've been to our birthday parties and weddings and my grandpa's funeral; they visited Libby when she was in the hospital. Jesús and Antonio taught me to play soccer when I was five years old, and Hilario cooks the greatest beefsteak dinner. Macario came here the year I was born and has come back every year since."

Alexa grabbed a breath and kept going. "We've visited them on their ranches and they butchered a goat in our honor. We've met them in Guanajuato for Christmas. They've named their babies for my dad and my grandpa." She halted. It looked like she was going to cry.

Jeff swallowed hard. He wasn't sure if he should feel bad or be angry at her for the lashing. "Okay," he said evenly. "I get the message."

"TOP POTS." The small metal sign hung above the toilet. Jeff almost laughed. *Give me a break. This place stinks. Geezuz, doesn't anyone know how to shut a toilet lid?*

He stepped outside and drew in a breath of air, then turned the water spigot and washed his hands. A man was drinking from the opposite end of the plastic tank. Water splashed in mud puddles at both ends, splattering over Jeff's leather boots and the man's worn tennis shoes.

"*Hola,*" the guy said, wiping his mouth on his shirtsleeve. He smiled, his tiny black mustache wrinkling up.

Jeff nodded. He knew what his father would say. "Why don't these people learn English? If I went to Mexico, I'd have to learn Spanish."

He yawned and glanced at the field. It seemed everyone had gone into slow motion. A couple of kids were laying in their rows, flipping berries at each other. Some of the workers sang a quiet Spanish song.

"Why don't you like him?" Libby's voice carried as he approached the truck. "It's completely obvious, Alexa. You're acting like a major jerk."

Jeff stopped at the cab door.

"You would, too, if it was *your* field he'd destroyed."

"It's not just your field, in case you forgot. It's a family farm, remember?"

"Yes, smarty, but I planted it for my ag-science class. Mr. Temple had to come out and look at it."

"He's not going to grade you down for something you didn't do. Besides, Jeff didn't destroy the entire field. Just a tiny part."

"Yeah, the part everyone can see from the road."

"All I know is, Jeff McKenzie is hot. Check out those brown eyes. And tell me you haven't noticed his rear. Does he fit those Levi's or what? I wonder how he'd look in Wranglers."

Jeff leaned against the door, trying not to laugh.

"A bit young to be looking, aren't you?" Alexa asked curtly.

"Don't tell me what to do. You think you're so perfect, Alexa, but guess what? You're not. I remember when you were in the sixth grade, you had a major crush on Todd Campbell. That's all we ever heard about. 'Oh—sigh—Todd is just toooo cute. Ohhh, Todd Campbell said hi to me today.'"

"Yeah, well, he was only in eighth grade. Jeff is probably five or six years older than you."

"There's no law against looking."

Chapter 4

THE AFTERNOON PUSH. Ethel was right. Jeff could hear her voice getting louder as the hours wore on, prodding, cajoling, threatening. She separated a number of boys, putting them at opposite ends of their rows. "Now you kids pick, or just forget coming back tomorrow."

"It's too hot," one complained.

"You haven't *seen* hot," she snapped.

Jeff agreed. This was nothing compared to an August tennis match, the sun scorching down, blinding your serve, the heat searing up from the court. *That* was hot.

Alexa was in the field now, checking behind the kids, calling them back to forgotten fruit.

"What time is it?" someone whined.

"Time to pick."

And then, as if the spell had been broken, the field turned into a frenzy of activity.

"Like a horse heading for the barn," said Mrs. Hampton, walking up to the scales. "They know it's almost quitting time."

Macario arrived on a four-wheeler. *"Hola,"* he said, studying the truck. "It is a good job," he told Jeff.

"Thanks."

Macario climbed on the truck, and Jeff began hauling flats from the scales. The pickers hurried from their rows, carrying the heavy crates or pushing laden wheelies, then jogged back for more.

"Geez," said Jeff, as he watched a Mexican return with another load. "How much did he pick?"

"Lots." Alexa's face said 'I told you so.' She punched a ticket. "Just like Pablo here. He'll easily make eighty dollars today."

Pablo grinned. "*Sí.* Maybe more. Maybe a hundred dollar. I am very good picker."

"*Ayyyye,*" a man yelped as he turned too sharply from his row, his cart tipping. Flats crashed to the ground.

The other pickers laughed, then scrambled to scoop up the spilled berries and reload the man's flats. "*Gracias,*" he told them sheepishly as he moved to the end of the line.

Weighing, punching, lifting, stacking. Again and again. Over and over. The dull ache in Jeff's lower back seemed to spread with each bend; his arms begged for rest and he squinted his eyes against the afternoon glare. But worse were the blisters shouting from his fingertips.

Suddenly, they were finished. A breeze picked up, the cool air soothing on Jeff's sunburned neck. But the thought of the day finally coming to an end was even more refreshing.

The truck door slammed and Macario appeared with an armful of ropes. Silently he set the pile on the ground and grabbed the top rope. Holding one end, he tossed the coiled line high into the air, up and over the first row of flats. Then he looped the rope around a steel hook just below the rim of the truck.

Rope after rope soared through the air, cresting the

truck like a wave, then crashed to the ground.

"Now we tie," Macario told Jeff. The dry brown hands moved slowly, gracefully, pausing each time the rope looped or twisted or turned. Then, taking Jeff's left hand, Macario placed it at the top of a loop. "Always hold here while you pull rope with the other hand." Macario offered him the dangling rope and Jeff gave it a strong yank, the rough braid ripping through his hands.

"*Más*. You want very tight." Macario took the rope, braced a foot against the outer stack of berries, then jerked. He wrapped the rope around the hook two more times, stuffing the leftovers under the wooden pallet.

"You do with me." Macario handed Jeff a rope. Together they secured the truck, step by step, yank by yank, knot by knot. "*Muy bien*," praised Macario. "You are *muy fuerte*—very strong."

Jeff nodded gratefully.

"I just talked to Jake," said Mrs. Hampton, joining them. "Bad news. Venancio ran a stop sign in Sheridan and hit a car. He's okay, except for a swollen ankle, but now we're short a driver." She looked at Jeff. "My husband wants to talk to you." She handed him the radio, indicating the press-to-speak button.

Jeff swallowed hard. "Mr. Hampton, this is Jeff."

"Yeah, Jeff," came the voice. "We've got a problem. I need a licensed driver. Can you handle a truck?"

"Don't I need a special permit?"

"No."

Jeff sucked in a deep breath. "I can probably do it."

"No probablies, Jeff. I need a 'yes' or 'no.'"

"Yes." God, what am I getting into?

"Go to the cannery with Macario. He'll show you what to do. Unit one clear."

Jeff handed the radio to Mrs. Hampton. "Unit nine clear," she said and returned the radio to her belt. "Well, looks like you two are off to Salem."

"*Sí*," said Macario.

Jeff jerked open the passenger door and stared at the tangle of ropes, an old burlap sack, smudged receipts, and a rusty coffee can filled with nails and bolts. He pushed aside a pair of leather work gloves and sank into the cracked, lumpy upholstery. "How long will this take?"

"*No sé*, maybe two hour. Is *problema*?"

"I need to practice."

"What you practice?"

"Tennis."

"You don't need practice today. You are strong from working."

"I'm a lot more sore than I am strong." Jeff rubbed his shoulder.

"You have Ben-Gay?"

"No—I'm usually in shape."

"Is good for the bad muscles."

Macario started the truck, shifted gears, and headed slowly down the crossroad and then along the south edge of the field.

"*Es necesario* to be in lowest gear when you drive in field."

The gear diagram had worn off the handle leaving only a dull black finish. "You line up with windshield wiper button." Macario pointed to a small silver knob on the dashboard.

The truck creaked as it dipped and swayed through a shallow ditch. Jeff held his breath, sure the load was going to slip. Macario crept onto the gravel road, shifted into second, gained a little speed, and moved into third gear.

Jeff's eyes wandered across the faded dashboard. He choked. "We're out of gas."

"No, the needle, it is broken." Macario tapped the gas gauge.

Jeff sighed and slumped back against the hot vinyl.

"*Muy sabrosa.*" Macario nodded to the long hedge-like rows on both sides of the road. The thick brambles were covered with small white blossoms. "Very much flavor."

"What are they?"

"In a few weeks, they are the boysenberries." He smiled. "Then Mrs. Hampton, she makes a pie for me."

At the grain tanks, a cloud of dust billowed around a large truck and trailer. A steady, golden stream poured into the truck from a cannon-like tube. Mr. Hampton stood on the cab step, giving a thumbs up as they drove by.

They passed a field where two men were unloading irrigation pipe from a metal trailer. Macario waved. The men grinned and nodded, keeping their hold on the aluminum pipe. "*Mis hermanos,*" he told Jeff. "My brothers, Santiago and Jerónimo."

Avoiding a string of potholes, Macario moved to the center of the road, and the truck settled into a steady rumble. Jeff rolled down the window, the stiff handle jerking in his hand. A breeze swept in from off a green field, the plants' silvery tips bowing in unison. Another field had been harvested, leaving a short, leafy stubble. Still another field had been cut and the grass lay in long, mounded rows.

A brown speckled hawk swooped down from a nearby telephone pole. As it dipped and swayed and climbed, three swallows appeared out of nowhere, darting at the larger bird, poking at its wings and body.

"I know just how you feel, buddy," Jeff muttered.

Turning onto the paved county road, Macario coaxed

the truck to forty-five miles an hour. Jeff wondered if this was max speed and figured at that rate it'd be midnight before he made it home.

"I get you a Coke, *¿sí?*" Macario asked when Martha's Market came into view.

"Sure, I guess, thanks." Jeff wished they could just keep going.

"Ah, you're looking better," Martha told Jeff as the screen door slammed behind him. "Must be the peppermint, or was it the *vaca rosa*?" She broke into a smile, her dark red lips outlining white teeth. Jeff looked at Macario.

"It means pink cow—you have milk and Pepto-Bismol for the *estómago*?"

"Yeah, that's what I had."

Macario set two Cokes on the counter along with a tube of Ben-Gay.

"What's the matter, Macario?" asked Martha, her penciled eyebrows coming together in a frown. "You workin' too hard?"

"No, is for Jeff."

"Geez, honey, what's the matter now?" She winked at him.

"Nothing."

Back in the truck, Macario handed Jeff the Ben-Gay. "It will start helping."

Traffic across the Center Street bridge was heavy. Macario crept to the stoplight, shifted to neutral, and put on the brake.

"Hey, berry boy!" a voice bellowed up.

Jeff groaned and looked down. Aaron Halvorson.

"We're taking a break before practice. Wanna go to

BJ's with us?"

"I wish, but we've gotta deliver these stupid berries to the cannery."

Steve Hailey leaned out the back window. "You gonna make the Hillsboro tournament?"

"Who knows."

"Hey, partner, I'm counting on you." Jason Gearhardt pushed Steve aside.

"Don't count too hard."

"Whatdaya mean? We're a team."

"I don't know if I can get Saturday off. I'll call you."

"Cindy Swartz is having a party tonight," said Aaron.

Traffic started to move and the truck began turning the corner. "I'm not sure what time we'll be back," Jeff hollered.

"Get that wetback driver of yours to step on it!" Aaron yelled back, then laughed.

Chapter 5

A HEAVY, SWEET AROMA HUNG in the warm air as Macario drove onto the cannery scales.

"That's good!" A woman with red hair crammed into a white hair net leaned out a small building. "Hampton Farms, right?"

"*Sí.*"

"Variety?"

"Totems."

"Looks like you have a full load today."

"*Sí*, almost."

Jeff watched in the side mirror as she walked around the truck, stapling rectangular pieces of white paper to each pallet. "Okay, I've got you tagged and weighed. You're behind the Oberg's semi. They should be about done. Go ahead, pull onto the receiving dock."

"*Muy bien.*"

Maneuvering around a wide turn, Macario avoided giant stacks of wooden pallets and rows of steel barrels. A forklift driver was positioning empty flats onto the end of a large truck.

"We will untie now." Macario turned off the engine.

What a waste. To undo what had taken so long to do. Jeff loosened the first knot. He coiled the rope and flung it over the truck. He winced. The yellow stacks blurred and his mind rested on one thought: I'm going to be really ticked if this job screws up my tennis game.

"Are you guys ready?" shouted the forklift driver above the noise of the starting semi.

Jeff nodded.

Moving in on his target, the driver slipped the dagger-like steel prongs into the pallet slots. Four stacks of fruit wobbled as he gently lifted, backed, and lowered his cargo. With a warning horn blast he approached a large opening in the concrete building marked "cooler," curtained with heavy strips of black plastic.

"That honking is going to drive me crazy," Jeff told Macario as it continued with each pass.

"Ah, *sí*, I have bad dream last night with that sound." Macario handed Jeff a rope to wind up. "I dream I am in Mexico and it is raining very hard and the river is coming up. The horn is warning for a flood."

Jeff studied the orange and black rope as he looped it around his hand. "You live by a river?"

"*Sí, Río Turbio*. It floods maybe two times in my life."

"Did it wipe out your house?"

"No, but big *problema*. *Mi casa*, it is made of adobe and the waters melt part of the walls. And the streets, they are dirt, so the mud goes into our house."

"What'd you do?"

"We stay with our friends in Cuerámaro, maybe eight kilometers away. When the flood is finished, we go back, and clean and clean. Much work. But, we are thankful nobody is hurt."

The forklift began loading empty flats onto the truck. Jeff reached for a rope piled on the asphalt.

"Is very important tie tight," advised Macario. "The empty flats, they get out too easy. I know." He laughed, pointing at himself. "I leave trail along road my first time."

With the truck tied down once again, they returned to the scales. "That's 16,320 pounds," said the redhead, handing Jeff a weight slip.

"Is that good?" Jeff asked Macario.

"*Sí*, for first picking Totems. We do better second time. Now you drive truck back."

"Already? Today?" Drive this piece of junk through Salem traffic? What if it stalled? Or had a flat tire? The entire load would probably slide off in the middle of the Marion Street bridge.

"See, you do okay," Macario said as Jeff edged into traffic. There was a reassuring steadiness to his voice.

"Yeah, well, let me know if you see any flying flats." Jeff's eyes darted from one side mirror to the other checking the roped stacks and noting the traffic alongside and behind the truck. It wasn't until they reached Martha's Market that he felt somewhat under control.

"You want *otra* Coke?" Macario asked.

"No, thanks. I just want to get home."

"You will practice tonight?" Macario looked at his watch.

"I'm gonna try."

"I don't know tennis. In Mexico, it is for the rich persons. We play soccer. Everyone can play, anywhere—in the parks or fields. Even in the street. Just put two rocks or sticks where the net should be."

"What about cars?"

"We yell '*aguas*'—watch out! Be careful! That is not just for a car coming but also if we are hitting too much the houses. Many broken windows with soccer. No *prob-*

lema for tennis, *¿sí?* You have the big fences around the tennis field?"

"Yeah, big fences, all right. We don't break too many windows."

"The houses in Mexico they have the bars over the windows—not just for bad peoples, but for bad soccer playing." Macario chuckled.

The last few miles seemed to take forever. Jeff felt himself going faster and faster, then backing off. He hated to drive like that—fast, slow, jerk, jerk, throw up. Finally, he approached the field entrance and kept to a steady crawl as the truck eased through the ditch and leveled out onto solid ground.

"Where do you want this parked?"

"Right side of the crossroad," said Macario. "We must unload the flats in many places."

"We're going to unload now?" Was it possible that his last shred of time was going to vanish?

"*Sí. Es necesario.* But you don't worry. You practice the tennis. Santiago will help."

As soon as he turned off the truck's ignition, Jeff hopped out of the cab. "See you later."

"*Sí. Hasta mañana.*"

Jeff jogged to his car. It was seven o'clock. He'd be on the courts by eight. But what about Debbie? And Cindy's party?

★ ★ ★

"Hi, Deb." Jeff eased back on his pillow, phone pressed to his ear, and stared at the ceiling.

"Hi, farmer boy."

"Be nice."

"I am nice. I think this is really cute. My boyfriend— the man of the land."

44

"You sound like Mark." He stretched his legs out and felt them relax. "Hope you didn't want to go to Cindy's, but I really had to practice tonight—if you can call it that."

"I didn't need to be around a bunch of people, not with our giant sale starting tomorrow. It's going to be a zoo for the next few days."

"Good. Then I don't have another angry person to add to my list."

"Who's angry?"

"Mark, for one. I missed picking him up from baseball practice. His coach had to bring him home."

"Who else?"

"Hampton's daughter. Guess I drove around in her school project. She barely talks to me."

"And just how old is this farmer's daughter?"

"I don't know. Fifteen. Sixteen. Actually, Deb, the other daughter is the one to worry about. She's really after me."

"And how old is *she*?"

Jeff waited.

"Jeffery—how old?"

"Ten, maybe eleven. Braces and all."

"You tease," Debbie scolded. "All right now, I haven't seen you in two days. How about tomorrow night?"

"I'll try. I don't know this farm schedule yet, or if there is such a thing. And then, practice—"

"Jeff McKenzie, you know I don't like third place."

Chapter 6

JEFF LOOKED AT HIS CLIPBOARD. "Danny Stevens?"

"You got that right, buddy."

Same kid, same trashy mouth, same hair in his eyes.

"You didn't finish your row yesterday." Jeff put a mark by Danny's name. "Go back to section two, row twenty-three."

"But I did finish." He spit on the ground. "Besides, the berries were too small. We don't have to pick the small ones."

Jeff took in a deep breath. Did he really have to deal with this little twerp again? Wasn't this Ethel's job? "I said row twenty-three. NOW!"

"Geezuz, man, don't have an attack." Danny kicked his empty flat, then slowly bent to pick it up. He rolled his eyes for his friends. "Come see me."

The strawberry harvest had moved to section three—to the Bentons—which presented a logistics problem. With the slower pickers still straggling through section two, weigh stations had to be split up. Libby took section two, Alexa section three. Ethel and Mrs. Hampton divided up, too, spreading themselves pretty thin.

Now there were two varieties to load. Macario had come by first thing that morning to warn Jeff. "Keep the berries apart. Load the Totems last."

The Bentons added another frustration: They didn't ripen evenly. A red berry, when turned over, might be light orange or even white.

"No *blanco*—no white," Alexa told the pickers again and again, holding up a sample. "Please be more careful."

Jeff was beginning to see the flatbed as his escape. Just load the crates, one on top of the other. No whiny kids, no rows to check, no one babbling in Spanish. He could pause, stretch, look around the farm and over to the Coast Range. Once in a while, though, his gaze would move across the berry field, past the gravel road, to the bean field. Alexa's dumb bean field. A reminder. Just like Mrs. Lambert's window he'd broken when he was nine years old. Bad enough he had to pay for it. Then he had to walk past it every day on the way to school.

Jeff watched now as someone crossed the bean rows to the irrigation line and stepped up to the motor platform. In a moment, the giant wheels began inching forward, moving the entire length of pipe and sprinkler heads through the swath of dark, moist ground.

"Lunch!" Ethel marched down the crossroad, her flowery shirt half untucked, her straw hat flopping. "Weigh your flats."

Libby and Mrs. Hampton came over from section two. Ethel pulled out her folding chair and Alexa sat on the ground in the shade of empty flats. Jeff grabbed his cooler from his car, rolling down the windows against the afternoon heat.

Libby pointed to the spot next to her on the flatbed, and Jeff wondered if he had a permanent lunch partner.

He opened his cooler. On top was a teddy bear sticky note. *"Dear Jeffery, Don't forget to ask for Saturday off. Love, Mom."*

"What's that?" Libby leaned over.

Jeff crumpled the paper. "Nothin'."

"Love letter?"

"Yeah—from my mom."

"Your mom makes your lunch?" Her eyes widened.

"I guess."

"Oh, poor baby, can't make his own lunch—"

"Libby." Mrs. Hampton shook her head.

"Just kidding." Libby held up her sandwich. "I made peanut-butter-and-jelly. I'll make you one tomorrow." She looked hopeful.

"That's okay." He glanced around the group, took a sip of pop, then asked Mrs. Hampton, "What's our work schedule for the next few days?"

Ethel yawned. "Long hours in the hot sun."

"Well," said Mrs. Hampton hesitantly, "it's hard to know. Let's see. Today's Thursday. With luck, we might finish section two by early afternoon, then we'll have everyone in the Bentons. I'd love to finish sections three and four tomorrow, then give the pickers the weekend off." She raised her eyebrows in question.

"I was wondering, that is, if it'd be okay, could I have Saturday off? I have a tennis tournament in Hillsboro."

She pursed her lips. "I don't know, Jeff. You've barely worked two full days." She bent down to retie her workboots.

"I know. I'm sorry, but I really need to be there. If there's any chance . . . "

"Let me radio Jake. I'll see what he thinks."

Jeff studied the ground as she explained the request to her husband.

The response came back with a swift kick. "Damn it. Why can't these kids work anymore? I told him it's a full-time job."

"There's a good chance we'll finish the first pick tomorrow," said Mrs. Hampton calmly.

The radio was silent.

"Jake?"

"I hear you. I don't know. You're running the show, you decide. The semi sounded funny yesterday. I gotta take it into Charlie's."

"I'll see you tonight. Unit nine clear."

"Unit one clear."

Mrs. Hampton set the radio in her lap and looked at Jeff. "How soon do you need to know?"

"My doubles partner will croak if I bag out at the last minute. I should call him tonight."

She studied the berry field. "Well, if we push hard and stay late, we can probably do it. Go ahead."

"Thanks. Thanks a lot."

Ethel gave him a thumbs-up. Alexa had been watching. She quickly looked away.

"Want a piece of licorice?" Libby dangled a long red cord in front of him.

"No thanks," Jeff said absently, thinking now of tennis. Who would his opponents be? Would he be ready? Would he have time to practice?

"Hey. Anybody gonna weigh my berries?" Danny Stevens lifted two flats onto the scale and pulled a ticket from his pocket. "That makes four." He grinned.

"Pretty good," said Alexa, rising to her feet. She punched his ticket. "Keep it up."

"When do I get my money?"

"You'll get a check next Wednesday," said Mrs. Hampton from her camp stool.

"Next Wednesday! I gotta wait that long?"

"We pay once a week."

"What a rip. You should pay every day."

"Sorry. We don't have the time." She stood and arched her back. "Besides, waiting will give you a bigger check."

Danny scoffed and tromped back to a friend standing in the middle of the field. The other kid pointed to the lake. Danny glanced back, catching Jeff's eye, then knocked his friend's arm down. They began punching at each other, then sauntered toward the outhouse.

"He's a jerk." Libby gnawed off a piece of red rope.

"You know him?" asked Mrs. Hampton.

"Yeah. He's in my class. He's always calling me rich—says we're rich farmers."

Mrs. Hampton chuckled. "That would be nice."

"I can't believe he picked four flats before lunch." Libby wiped her mouth. "He's such a screw-off."

Mrs. Hampton twisted her head, looking back to section two. "Libby, did you mark the flats like I asked?"

Libby stopped chewing. "Oh, shoot." She strained to see the stacks of fruit waiting to be loaded. "I did ten to a stack and put an empty on top. Do you think—?"

Mrs. Hampton shrugged. "I'd go check." She took a large black marking pen from the cash box. "Better do it now before it's too late."

Libby hopped down, snatched the marker, and ran to her scale.

No one spoke for a few minutes. Ethel shut her eyes and pulled her hat over her face. Alexa began rolling her T-shirt sleeves over her shoulders. The front said "It's Your Turn," with a big wave splashing around the words.

"We're missing one!" Libby announced between gasps. "I'll bet it was that Danny Stevens. He takes stuff at school."

Everyone scanned the field.

Jeff closed the lid to his cooler and slipped off the truck. He casually walked to the outhouse, knocked, then opened the door. "Geezuz."

"They plugged the urinal," he told Mrs. Hampton, "with a giant wad of toilet paper. There's a yellow lake in the bottom."

"Great. Keep an eye out for those two," she told everyone. "We'd better get moving if we want to finish tomorrow." Then she asked Jeff, "Would you unclog the urinal?"

Libby scrunched her nose. "Oh, Mom, that's not fair."

"Would you like to help?"

"No way."

"I'll use one of those wire flags," said Jeff.

When he returned to the truck, Alexa's face hinted a smile. "Fun, huh?"

"Yeah. Most fun I've had in days."

As Jeff hoisted himself onto the flatbed, he heard a forlorn voice. "Someone stole my berries."

He looked down at a young girl, her hair straggling around her face and shoulders, berry stains on her knees and tears in her eyes.

"Whatdaya mean, someone stole your berries?"

"My flat was gone after lunch."

Alexa put her arm around her. "That's too bad, Sarah, but don't you remember? Always weigh in your berries before you go to lunch, or take them with you. Most everyone's pretty honest out here, but there's always a creep or two."

Now the tears ran down Sarah's dusty face. "My mom said I had to pick four flats or I'll be in trouble."

Alexa looked up to Jeff. "Could you get me a flat?"

Jeff knelt down with an evenly filled crate.

"Better weigh it," Alexa told Sarah.

Sarah lowered her eyes and mumbled, "Thank you." She set the flat on the scale and handed Alexa a tattered ticket.

"That's fifteen pounds," said Alexa in a soothing voice, punching the ticket. "Be more careful, okay?"

Sarah nodded and shuffled back to her row.

Once more Jeff started to load the truck, when his eye caught sight of his car. The driver's door was open. Had he forgotten to shut it? He stared for a moment, then jumped down.

"What's wrong?" asked Alexa.

"Nothing—I hope."

A gaping hole glared at Jeff from where his CD player should have been. His jaw clenched as he turned in a circle and scoured the field. His eyes stopped at the thicket of green cattails lining the lake's edge, their spiked leaves swaying in the breeze. Wait a minute. There was no breeze. Jeff studied the cattails as they moved in a steady rhythm—away from the field.

He sprinted across section two, leaping the berry rows like low hurdles.

"Go, go!" shouted a picker. Someone applauded.

Hitting the grassy strip at the rear of the field, he turned and ran along the edge of a cornfield. Water from an irrigation sprinkler cascaded overhead. His breath came hard now and his legs ached with the strain of his boots. But the thought of his CD player sent a flash of anger and a shot of adrenaline through his body. He jumped a small ditch and ran past heavy wooden posts anchoring the boysenberry rows. Faster, he urged, faster. They're heading for the road. Come on, beat them to it.

At last, the cattails faded into a shallow marsh. Jeff staggered to a stop, leaned over, and gasped for breath.

His heart pounded in his dry throat. The cattails rustled. Jeff quickly raised up. Out walked Danny Stevens and his buddy.

"What are you guys up to?" Jeff tried to fake authority along with a normal breathing pattern.

"Gettin' outta here," Danny's friend said.

The boys moved toward the road.

"What's in your shirt?" Jeff stepped forward.

"None of your stinkin' business," said Danny.

"How about a CD player?" Jeff took another step, reaching for the object.

Danny yanked it out, held it up, then flung it into the lake. "Go get it, Mr. Detective." He broke for the road.

Jeff dived for Danny's legs, knocking him to the ground. Danny squirmed and kicked. Jeff hung on as they rolled to the water. Now the other guy was kicking Jeff's arms. Letting go, Jeff rose to his knees, but a foot smacked into his chest and he fell backward, landing on his shoulder.

The sound of a four-wheeler jolted the air. Danny raced to the road. Jeff's assailant paused for a split second. Jeff jumped to his feet and wrestled him to the ground. The four-wheeler burst out of a boysenberry row and sped after Danny. A moment later, Macario returned with Danny in a headlock.

"You stinkin' wetback," screamed Danny. "Get your dirty rotten hands off me!"

Jeff pulled the other boy to his feet.

"I ain't done nothin'," the kid yelled.

Breathing deeply, Jeff looked at Macario. "Thanks."

Macario grinned. "Alexa radioed—say maybe you need help."

"Alexa say right."

Chapter 7

A BROWN DATSUN STORMED into the berry field, crashing over ruts and swerving around potholes. As it approached the crossroad, Mrs. Hampton walked briskly out of a nearby row. Danny Stevens and his buddy, Eric Wilson, stood up from their assigned detention post against a truck tire.

Jeff watched from the flatbed as the driver's door flung open. A man wearing broad orange suspenders pulled himself out and slammed the door. He marched toward the boys, his striped work shirt jerking out of his faded jeans. "What the hell's going on?" It was the same guy who'd yelled at Danny the other morning.

Before anyone could answer, he grabbed Danny's arm. "I had to leave the steel mill to come get you." Danny yanked his arm free.

Mrs. Hampton cleared her throat. "As my husband explained to you on the phone, Mr. Stevens, these boys were caught stealing and running away from the field."

"Listen, lady, you're supposed to be watching them." He pulled a greasy red handkerchief from his pocket and wiped his face.

"Mr. Stevens, we have close to a hundred pickers out here. It's impossible to keep an eye on every one of them." She gripped her clipboard. "We must have responsible people in our fields, but that apparently does not include your son or his friend."

"I've been watching them." Jeff jumped from the truck.

"Who are you?" Stevens jammed the handkerchief back into his pocket.

"Take it easy, Mr. Stevens," said Mrs. Hampton. "This is Jeff McKenzie, from Salem. He's working for us this summer."

"So the Sheridan kids aren't good enough for you, huh?" He kicked the ground with his boot, stirring the dust.

Ignoring him, Mrs. Hampton flipped the papers on her clipboard. "When Jeff gets me a receipt for a new CD player, I'll mail it to you. Once we receive payment, I'll send the boys' checks."

"Hell, lady, don't you give anyone a second chance?"

"*Mis*-ter Stevens," she said firmly, "they were stealing. They're lucky I didn't call the sheriff. But I will if you continue this conversation."

"What a two-faced operation," he growled, pointing around the field. "Just look out there—full of Mexicans. Everyone knows wetbacks will steal you blind."

"Just one minute." Mrs. Hampton spoke with acid clarity. "You have no right to speak of these people like that. Many of them have worked for us for years. They are honest folks trying to earn a decent living."

"Then you'd better keep them in the fields," snapped Stevens. "Next thing ya know, they'll be after my job!" He spun around, signaling the boys to follow.

Mrs. Hampton took off her straw hat and fanned her face. "Can you believe that?"

Libby was wide-eyed.

Alexa walked over and gave Mrs. Hampton a hug. "Nice goin', Mom. You told him."

"I'm shaking," she said, taking a deep breath.

A sense of relief filled the rest of the afternoon. Jeff felt it and he could see it in the others. Alexa seemed friendlier. Her eyes would actually meet his when they spoke. Mrs. Hampton and Ethel breezed through the field, urging everyone to stay later with promises of the weekend off.

But Jeff's body tensed again when Macario handed him a rope and said something about another trip to the cannery. "Venancio, his foot is still too big. He cannot drive."

"Debbie isn't going to like this."

"Who?" Macario paused.

"Debbie, my girlfriend."

"Oh, the *novia*. *Es un problema*." He leaned against the door. "My wife, she is in Mexico, so I have no *problema*. I can work many hours, many days. Then I send *mucho dinero* to *mi familia*."

"How long are you here?"

"Maybe nine month."

"That'd be too long for my girlfriend," said Jeff, shaking his head. "She couldn't handle the two weeks I was in Palm Springs last Christmas."

"We send many *cartas* and photographs." He reached to his back pocket and pulled out a tattered wallet. "I just must be home in *octubre*. I have new baby in *noviembre*." He carefully removed several small photos from the wallet. "Eduardo—he is fifteen."

Jeff hadn't figured Macario's age, but he didn't seem old enough to have a fifteen-year-old son. The picture wasn't any better than most school photos here, but it would help if the kid smiled.

"Alejandra, she is thirteen. Tomas is ten and Ruben is eighteen *meses*."

"What about your wife?" asked Jeff.

"She is Teresa. But I have no *fotografía*."

"Better get one or you'll forget what she looks like."

"I will not forget." Macario returned his wallet to his pocket and opened the cab door.

Jeff sighed. He felt like he was in a giant hole, trying to climb out, but his hands and feet kept slipping.

Chapter 8

JEFF LOOKED DOWN THE LENGTH of empty tennis courts. Sunlight gleamed bright against the long row of taut, white-trimmed nets. Early morning shadows stretched across the green asphalt. How would he do today, he wondered with such a short practice last night? And there was the dull pain in his shoulder, a nagging reminder of his encounter with Danny Stevens. Would the pain flare up?

"Come on, McKenzie, let's warm up," said Jason Gearhardt, tossing Jeff a ball.

With easy, sweeping strokes, Jeff hit from the baseline, returning shot after shot, scooting to the left for a backhand and jogging to the net for a series of volleys. He breathed the intoxicating smell of warming courts and the sharp, tangy scent of new tennis balls. God, he loved this game—the jerky squeaks of braking, skidding tennis soles, the solid whack of balls meeting firm nylon strings, the spectator shouts and claps.

"Okay, let's get started," called the Hillsboro pro.

Jason and Jeff moved off their court, falling in with

Aaron Halvorson and his doubles partner, Steve Hailey.

"Hey, berry boy, how can I get hands like these?" Aaron grabbed Jeff's right hand, examining the stains on his fingers and the dark lines beneath his nails. "Let me read your palm, my boy. Aha! A long life—on a muddy road!"

Jeff yanked his hand free. What was it with Aaron, anyway? Sometimes he was pretty easy going. But other times he'd act strangely aloof, barely saying "hi" in the halls and practically ignoring Jeff during a game. Even his humor could turn to biting sarcasm.

When word had spread at school about Jeff's farm job, Aaron had stopped him in the bathroom. "Tough luck, man. I was planning on some deadly games this summer. And what a bum deal for all those club women who think you're such a stud."

"Get real, would ya, Halvorson?" Jeff had grumbled.

Aaron flexed an arm. "Guess I'll just have to take your place."

"Whatever turns you on."

Now, Jeff decided to keep it light. "You want hands like mine? Just come on down, and we'll give you a row of your very own. Pick strawberries all day and the hands are yours."

"No way, José," protested Aaron. "What would my tennis students think?"

"Who cares?" said Jeff as they joined the group.

Aaron wouldn't shut up. "So what does Debbie say about your new lifestyle? You didn't make it to Cindy's party the other night."

"We were busy."

"Knowing Debbie, she would have made time to party," Aaron smirked. "You're not taking very good care of your lady."

Jeff bristled. "I said we were busy. She was getting ready for some big sale, and I had to practice. So back off. She's not your worry."

"She'll be your worry if you don't give her more attention. Or would you rather spend time with those beaners?"

"Geezuz, Aaron, give it a rest."

The Hillsboro pro cleared his throat. "You probably remember most everyone from last summer. I'll let you introduce yourselves on the courts. We've got some fine participants here today—a few ranked in the Northwest Top Twenty. Good luck to each of you, and we've got some nice little trophies this year."

Jason nudged Jeff. "Hey, Mr. Ranked, you going for one of those 'nice little trophies'?"

"Yeah, right. I'm proudly ranked right near the bottom and falling fast."

"Hey, that's better than me with no ranking at all."

"Stay in school, study hard, and maybe someday the golden number will be yours."

"Mr. McKenzie—are you with us?"

Jeff looked up. "Yeah."

"You'll be on court number two in a singles match with Brian McEvers. Go ahead and get started. Remember, this is no-ad scoring. First point after deuce is the winner. And try to avoid split sets—I don't want to go through too many new balls."

Jeff had played Brian a number of times over the years. Should be a win, he figured, twirling his racket in his hand.

Brian's first serve proved Jeff wrong. Ace. Jeff shook his head in disgust. "Get your rear in gear," he warned himself.

"Fifteen-love. Service," Brian called as he threw the ball in the air.

Jeff hopped back and forth on his feet, anticipating the hit. A hundred miles an hour, he calculated as the ball screamed across the net. Tensing, he held his breath and met the target with a compact backswing, sending the ball back to baseline. A few more deep shots and Jeff began breathing easier. That's it. Another baseline, then let's force a short ball.

Jeff hit his next shot crosscourt. Brian raced to meet the bounce, stretched, and barely got it over the net. Jeff had already charged forward, set his position, and kissed the ball with a crisp volley into Brian's right front court. Yes! Perfect placement. Brian didn't even try for the return. There was that sweet rush of adrenaline.

"Fifteen all. Service."

The sun rose higher and Jeff felt his eyes squinting as the games slipped by. He won the first set, six games to Brian's four. But now he was down in the second set, three to five. He could tell he was losing his momentum. His legs were tired and his shoulder throbbed. Racing for a wide baseline hit, he met the ball late, sending it into the next court.

"Hey, McKenzie, watch it!" shouted Aaron, tossing the ball back.

Jeff swung his racket through the air. Timing. That was it. His timing was off. Confirming his diagnosis were two sloppy high returns which Brian killed. Jeff felt sick.

Losing the set, he dropped onto his bench. He took a long drink of Gatorade while Brian went for new balls. "Come on, get with it," he urged himself, looking around the courts. "You can beat this guy."

Back on the court, Jeff swung his racket through the air. A stabbing pain flashed through his shoulder. Despite his pep talk, the thought of losing stayed with him. He managed a decent top-spin lob, clearing Brian's rush to the net. That felt good. And he had a couple of ace serves and a few awesome volleys, but they weren't enough to counter his poor timing. His game slipped away.

"That's your set and match," Jeff called flatly as his last serve landed in the net.

"Thanks. Nice match," Brian said as he reached across the net to shake Jeff's hand.

"Yeah, right. Congratulations," Jeff mumbled.

His afternoon doubles match seemed cut from the same mold. With Jason as his partner, they took on Hillsboro's number one team.

"Sorry, Jason, I'm really out of sync today," Jeff apologized as they lost the first set.

"That's okay, man, no problem. We'll get 'em next round."

Jason was right on, hitting great serves and charging the net.

"Awesome volley," Jeff said as Jason sliced a return straight down the middle.

Favoring his shoulder, Jeff failed to hit through his serves, sending the ball into the net or glancing off the tape.

"Come on, Jeff, you can do it," said Jason.

"I know, I know. Sorry."

But it still wasn't there and, packing his bag, Jeff apologized again. "I really lost it for us, Jason. Sorry. I don't know what my problem is. Guess it's the shoulder. Maybe you'd better look for another partner."

"No way. You just had an off day. We all have 'em. It was probably Halvorson. He's such an ass. Don't listen to him."

"Hard not to," grumbled Jeff.

"He's just jealous."

"Of what?"

"Of you, stupid." Jason took a drink of water, then splashed a handful on his hair. "You've always out-scored him on the courts." Jason rubbed his hair with a towel. "And he's lusted after every girl you've ever dated."

★　★　★

Turquoise waters lapped against the sparkling white tile of the Madrona Hills swimming pool.

"That's the best thing I've seen all day—how about a swim?" Jeff asked Jason as the club van pulled into the service parking lot.

"Your eyes need to be examined." Jason nodded to the bikinied bodies on the chaise longues. "Someone named Debbie is waving at you, dummy."

"How are ya, stranger?" she greeted Jeff at the pool gate.

"Lots better now." He bent to kiss her lips. "I knew I'd been missing something."

"What—me or my mouth?" She removed her sunglasses and slipped them into her dark hair.

"Your mouth, of course." He grinned, dropping his bag next to a large oak barrel filled with flowers.

"You reject." She hit his arm.

"Hey, careful, that's the bad one."

"Oh, poor baby, come over on the grass and I'll give you a back rub."

Jeff carefully slipped his shirt off as he knelt on the soft green lawn. "Ohhh," he groaned, "I ache all over." He lay down, sighing as he felt his body melt into the grass. Debbie's hands moved across his back, up his neck, and into his hair. He could smell her tanning lotion mixed with some sort of perfume.

"How'd it go at Hillsboro?" she murmured.

"Don't ask."

"You needed me there." She rubbed his shoulder.

"Easy," Jeff urged. "Your monster nails are scratching."

"Don't offend my fingernails. They represent a lot of tender, loving care. Besides, I broke one at the sale this morning—shut it in the cash register."

Jeff rolled over and pulled her to his chest. "Oh, disaster. Do you still make your commission with a broken fingernail or do you get a black mark?"

She bent down and kissed his lips. "You'd better be good or I won't give you the shorts I bought today."

"Let's go for a swim."

"You go." She smiled slyly. "I've got to work on my nail—I wouldn't want any black marks."

Chapter 9

"A *VACA ROSA* TO START YOUR MONDAY morning?" Martha asked.

"No, thanks." Jeff poured a cup of coffee.

"So," Martha said, taking his money, "how's it going?"

"Okay, I guess." He slipped the change into his pocket.

"Don't let Mr. Hampton hear you say 'I guess.'" She looked at him with her crossed eye. "That man does not like guessing. You either know or you don't know. 'Make a decision, right or wrong,' he always tells me."

"I'll remember that," Jeff muttered, pushing open the screen door. Great, just great. Add one more thing to the list: Do a good job, practice your tennis, keep your girlfriend happy, and—don't guess. He winced as hot coffee splashed on his hand.

Driving toward the Coast Range, he stared blankly at the irregular gray line set against the pale blue sky. He felt himself moving forward and the landscape moving back, but his mind seemed caught in between.

A hawk stood guard atop a telephone pole at the entrance to Bethel Road. It didn't budge, not even with the crunch of gravel as Jeff turned off pavement. Was it asleep? Or scouring the field for breakfast? Did hawks have to do anything except eat and sleep? Suddenly, it dropped from its roost, dived straight down, swooped back up, and soared out across the open field.

★　★　★

Another day in the strawberry patch, Jeff thought reluctantly, as the grain bins came into sight. With his poor showing at Hillsboro, he should be on the courts right now. He took in a deep breath and let it out slowly. That's when he saw the paint. He slowed down. Black paint. Sprayed all over the corner tank, spelling out in sloppy words "Wetbacks go home."

Cars lined both sides of the road, and a group of pickers waited near the stacks of empty flats. Big crowd today, Mrs. Hampton had predicted. Second pick in the Totems. Best of the season.

"Good morning," she said as he walked up to the truck.

"Morning. What happened to your grain tank?"

Her smile disappeared and her lips tightened. "We've had a lot of vandalism over the years, but this is the first graffiti." She sighed. "If someone has a gripe, I wish they'd come talk to us."

Jeff swallowed hard. What had Mrs. Hampton said the night of his vandalism? Was she waiting for an explanation? An apology?

He held out his hand. "Here's that receipt for my new CD player."

"Thanks, Jeff. I'll send a copy to Mr. Stevens. Hope we don't have any trouble."

Alexa looked to the road as another car pulled over. "We're going to have berries coming out of our ears today."

"I know," said Mrs. Hampton. "We'll have two loads." She glanced at Jeff. "Venancio still can't drive. Are you ready?"

"I guess." He paused. "I mean, yes."

Ethel marched up to the truck, a large thermos under one arm, her cooler in the other hand. "That is just spittin' awful," she snapped. "Who in their right mind would do such a thing? If I get my hands on them, I'll wring their wretched necks." She jammed her cooler under the truck.

"Fortunately, most of our pickers come the other way." Mrs. Hampton nodded down the road. "They may not see it."

"But still," said Ethel, "the nerve."

"They also stole the keys from the semi," said Mrs. Hampton. "Jake was like a caged lion. He stomped around the house looking for another set. It put him back forty-five minutes."

Ethel shook her head. Her hair had changed colors. Solid brown now, with sort of an orange shadow. "They even knocked over the Feldman's mailbox. Little brats."

"Where's Libby?" asked Jeff.

"You mean, speaking of brats?" said Alexa. "You catch on fast. She's asleep in Mom's pickup."

"Okay, troops," said Ethel, tying her straw hat, "let's head 'em up, move 'em out."

"Alexa," Mrs. Hampton called back, "I'd like you and Jeff to pick those berries for Mrs. Dixon."

Alexa groaned. "Mrs. Dixon is about ninety years old," she told him, "and still makes all her own jam. But she can't pick anymore, so guess who's elected?"

"Sorry, I don't know how."

"You've never picked strawberries?" she asked in disbelief. "One of those spoiled city kids, huh?"

Jeff cringed. "Wait a minute. Just because I live in Salem doesn't mean I'm spoiled. I suppose all country kids are perfect."

Alexa stared at him for a moment. Then she snapped to attention. "Listen, Jeff McKenzie, I never wanted you here in the first place. We got along fine without you, so why don't you just pack it up and go back to your fancy country club and hit tennis balls the rest of your life?" She grabbed a coffee can and an empty flat. "I've got berries to pick."

Jeff took a deep breath and leaned against the flatbed. Where did that come from? he wondered. Someone is a bit sensitive. He brushed a rotten berry off the truck. "Why don't you pack it up and go back?" The words echoed in his head. He looked down at his boots. The toes were scratched and mud lined the worn creases.

How had this gotten so complicated? Why *didn't* he just leave? Refuse to come back? Con his parents into paying off the debt? The thought, however, nagged at his gut. He looked out to the Coast Range, his eyes settling on a flat-topped ridge. Slowly, new words formed in his mind: He was wrong.

But how do you say them?

Jeff found another coffee can and walked slowly down the row. He knelt across from Alexa and picked a berry. *Kathunk*—into the can. "My folks gave me a tennis racket when I was six. That's been my summers ever since. I've never picked strawberries. But I have picked up lots of tennis balls. Does that count?"

Alexa rustled through the damp foliage. "Grab the cap and stem and, with your other hand, twist the berry off." The deep red fruit glistened in the palm of her hand. "Hold as many as you can before you dump them. It'll save time."

Jeff peered into the jungle of leaves and trailing vines. A cold wetness spread across his right knee. He glanced down. Mashed berry clung to his jeans.

"Be sure to pick the rotten ones. Just leave them in the aisle."

"You're not serious."

She tossed a hairy, gray berry at her feet. "If they end up in the flats, we get docked big time. And don't miss any red ones or you'll really be in trouble."

"With who—you or Ethel?"

"Ethel." Alexa finally looked at him. "She'll throw you on the ground and stuff berries down your throat. Rotten ones." A faint smile flickered across her lips.

They worked together in silence, moving along the row, pawing through the bushes, picking, and dumping.

"Hey, look at this one." Jeff held up a huge berry.

"When Libby and I were little," said Alexa, "we called those 'jackpots.'"

"It's doomed. I gotta eat it."

"The bigger ones are bland sometimes." She popped a perfect, small berry into her mouth.

Jeff watched her for a moment, then he picked a leaf and began tearing it apart. "Alexa?"

"Uh-huh."

"I, um." He yanked off another leaf. "I'm sorry about your bean field. I didn't know it was a school project."

"How'd you hear that?"

"You and Libby—talking about it the other day."

Alexa's eyes widened. "So, why did you do it?"

Jeff sat down. "I don't suppose you've ever driven around in some farmer's field."

"Are you crazy? My dad would kill me. Besides, I know all the farmers around here. I'd have to go to Eastern Oregon if I ever wanted to do something like that."

"Well, I didn't think anyone owned the field," Jeff said. "It was just land in the country—no fence, no gate, no sign. Besides, it was dark." Now he was grasping for excuses.

"Oh, so that's what we have to do," Alexa said, leaning back on her heels. "We're suppose to fence and gate and light everything, then put up a sign: Beans growing. Please do not disturb. Thank you so much, The Hamptons."

She started picking again. "What about the other kid? Why isn't he out here?"

"Can you keep a secret?"

"Maybe."

"Come on, promise?"

"Oh, all right."

"We were celebrating Paul's appointment to the Air Force Academy. If anyone finds out about this, they'll kick him out for sure."

"You're covering for him?"

"Uh-huh."

"Good friend?"

"Yeah."

"Well, that's real nice, Jeff McKenzie. I guess I'll have to give you ten points."

"Will that cover the bean field?"

"No way."

A picker walked behind Alexa with a full flat. "*Con permiso.*"

"*Pase.*" Alexa poured the berries from her coffee can into the flat. "This ought to be enough for Mrs. Dixon." She stabbed an orange marker flag into the row. "We'd better get back to the scale."

Once the pickers started bringing in their fruit, the pace didn't let up. Alexa woke Libby and coaxed her from the pickup. They quickly fell behind, flats piling up in careless stacks around the scales.

Jeff stopped loading the truck and just tended the scales, snatching flats off as quickly as Alexa and Libby punched tickets, setting the crates in neat rows behind them.

"Thanks," Alexa would say when she had a spare second or "sorry" as she turned blindly, bumping him with a full flat.

"Looks like the pickers are out to get us," he said.

During lunch, Macario drove another truck along the south edge of the field and parked it just past the crossroad. "We drive two trucks today."

"Yeah, I heard." Jeff grimaced.

Macario pulled an envelope from his shirt pocket. "I get *carta* from *mi esposa*."

"We say cards," Libby told him from her spot on the truck. "They have cute pictures on them. Did you get a card with a cute picture?"

"No. Is just writing on paper. But I have another paper with drawing from Tomas." He handed her the picture.

"What is it?"

"Is *caballo*, pulling wagon with sugarcane."

Mrs. Hampton took off her sunglasses and wiped them with her T-shirt. "What's new at home, Macario?"

"Nothing is new. The crops, they need the water. Especially the garbanzos. We should have rain by now."

"What about that river?" asked Jeff.

"It dries very low in the hot times. And we have no money for the pipes and the pumps. And no electricity. We just hope for the *tormentas*—the rain storms."

"Don't mention rain here," warned Mrs. Hampton. "Not until all our crops are in."

"Too bad we can't give Macario's family some of our water," said Libby.

Macario smiled. "*Muchas gracias*, Libby." He folded his letter and drawing and tucked them back in his pocket.

"How was your important competition?" he asked Jeff.

"Ugly."

"*Feo.*"

"That's my tennis game all right—*feo.*"

"When is another one?"

"Saturday—in Eugene. But if I don't practice, it'll be extremely *feo.*"

"I show you soccer exercise."

"Soccer?"

"*Sí.* Remember, I just know soccer. Maybe it helps your tennis. You stand in front of me."

Jeff moved reluctantly, wondering how this could really help.

"Is only a minute. Then you take a minute many times in the day to practice. It is very good for the quick body."

With his feet firmly planted, Macario began bobbing, left and right, up and down. Then just his head, twisting it right, left, up, down. "You follow me."

Jeff felt stupid, bouncing and jerking, unable to second-guess the next move, and it didn't help with everyone else laughing.

"Thanks a lot, you guys," he said between gyrations. "Why don't you try it?"

"That's okay," said Libby. "You look great."

Macario grinned broadly. "Don't forget—practice many times. Is good plan."

"Dad's here." Alexa pointed to the white pickup jostling to a stop near the second truck.

"He's not exactly all smiles," said Ethel, watching as

Mr. Hampton shut his pickup door.

"How was Portland?" asked Mrs. Hampton.

"Lousy. There were twenty-seven rigs in front of me." He picked a berry out of a flat and took a bite. "I've got to reload and get back this afternoon. There's a ship in from Egypt, but it's almost full. We could get chopped off."

"Have you called the sheriff on the grain tanks?"

"I haven't had time. Besides, graffiti isn't exactly a high priority crime." He examined the truck.

"We'll have two good loads today," said Mrs. Hampton.

He nodded, then looked at Jeff. "You ready to drive?"

"Sure," answered Jeff uneasily.

Mr. Hampton kissed his wife. "I'll see you sometime tonight."

"Have a safe trip."

"*Que le vaya bien*," said Macario, climbing onto the flatbed.

"*Gracias.*"

A few hours later, Macario moved the fully loaded Ford to the edge of the field and returned with the empty truck. "You go to the cannery now," he told Jeff.

"Aren't we going together?"

"Is not good for *fruta* to sit many hours in the sun. I stay here and load the GMC. Maybe I see you later."

"But what if I have problems?"

"Alexa," said Macario, "do you have *otra* radio?"

"There's another one in Mom's pickup." She hurried off and returned holding up the radio. "Unit ten."

Macario twisted a tiny black knob, and a short screech pierced the air. "To talk you push the side, here, and say the words at the top, but is not necessary to talk loud."

Jeff took the radio, examining the buttons. "Ten-four, good buddy," he said into the small speaker.

"No ten-four," warned Macario. "Is most important you say Mr. Hampton's numbers—WNWP836. Then you say your unit—ten. Then the unit who you call. If you want Alexa or Mrs. Hampton—"

"Or me," Libby called from her scale.

"Or Libby," Macario said, smiling. "You say 'unit ten to unit nine.' For me, you say 'unit three.' For Mr. Hampton, 'unit one.'"

Jeff climbed into the cab and patted the steering wheel. "Okay, baby, it's just you and me." He pushed in the clutch, pumped the gas pedal, and turned the key. A loud, steady rumbling filled the cab.

He drove easily along the edge of the field, crawled through the ditch, and picked up speed as he moved to the center of Bethel Road. He glanced at the passing fields. Water arched gracefully from sprinklers stretched across the newly sprouted cornfields. In the boysenberries, two gigantic sprinkler heads shot fire-hose sprays far into the air. Now, it seemed, the only thing in the world was the gravel road before him, rolling fields on either side, and a forever sky.

Chapter 10

A WOMAN IN A WHITE LAB COAT stepped from the cannery office. Wearing rubber gloves and holding a rectangular white pan, she waited as the forklift operator lowered the first stack of Hampton berries onto a wide, covered concrete slab. Then she began taking berries from the top flat and placing them into her pan.

"What are you doing?" Jeff asked.

"Grading your load."

"You judge the whole truck from just a couple of berries?"

"I try to get a good cross section," she said. "Let's go down a few more."

He set aside six flats and watched as she randomly selected a handful of berries.

"Oh," she said suddenly, "what have we here?"

Jeff stared into the crate. Dirt clods and rocks covered the bottom.

She raised an eyebrow. "Looks like you've got some dishonest pickers."

They found four more padded flats in the stack. After

inspecting the other stacks and finding nothing, Jeff asked, "Are you docking us?"

"No. I'm more concerned about the condition of the fruit. The rest of your sample looks really good—see?"

A mix of size and color filled her pan. A few caps and stems. One berry had a little rot on it. Jeff wanted to snatch it out.

"It's probably just one picker," said the inspector. "He—or she—brought them in all at once. You'd better get somebody to put a quick stop to it."

The forklift driver was loading empties as Jeff walked back to the truck. Standing off to the side, he watched as the driver moved pallets to the truck, stopped, returned to the stacks, stopped. Jeff realized his body was moving, keeping time. He looked carefully in all directions, then he began bobbing, twisting, and dodging an imaginary opponent.

Jeff checked the side-view mirrors for the hundredth time. He'd made it across the bridge, through West Salem traffic, and was now heading out of town. He glanced at the pink weight slip on the seat beside him and wondered how the Hamptons would react to the rock business. Was this just a small problem? Like the plugged urinal?

A horn honked. Jeff quickly looked in his left mirror. A burgundy van. Right mirror—nothing. But wait. Back alongside the road there was something yellow. Jeff stiffened and clutched the steering wheel. He glanced at the traffic in front, then eyed the right mirror again. Zing. A flash of yellow. Like a giant Frisbee. His heart climbed into his throat. God no, he pleaded.

He looked for a place to pull over. There was no real

shoulder. Maybe fifteen inches, and then mailboxes, shrubs, someone's yard. His mouth turned dry as he watched more flats fly into the air, crashing into the ditch or bouncing behind the truck. The burgundy van honked again as it plowed across a flat.

"I know, I know." His head throbbed and sweat slid down his neck. This was not part of the deal. If he had wanted to drive trucks, he would have applied at Pepsi.

Martha's Market finally came into sight. He flipped on his blinker, slowed, and turned. There, parked along the edge of the county road, was the GMC. Jeff looked around for Macario and pulled over.

"¡*Hola!*" Macario waved as Martha's screen door slammed behind him.

Jeff pushed open his door and stepped onto the running board. Holding the door for support, he reached tentatively for the pavement.

"You are okay?" asked Macario.

"*Sí,*" answered Jeff quietly.

"You want a drink?" Macario offered his Coke.

"Thanks."

Macario began inspecting the load, walking around the truck. Jeff held his breath.

"¡*Mala suerte!*"

A hollow feeling sucked at his stomach. He forced himself around the truck. An entire stack was missing, and another leaned precariously toward the vacant spot.

"They're along the highway." Jeff pointed grimly toward Salem. "At least one is smashed into a million pieces."

"Don't worry. Many drivers lose the empty flats. It is very easy." Macario nodded as if trying to convince Jeff. "We can tie the rest in. You will be happy."

"I don't have any more ropes."

Macario jogged over to the GMC and returned with a blue nylon rope. He climbed the iron rungs alongside the cab and crawled out across the stacks. Like a spider spinning a web, he moved the cord in and out of the ropes. He hopped down, slipped the rope under hooks, tossed it back over the load, and secured it.

As Macario rechecked all the lines and knots, untying, tightening, and retying, Jeff felt like a schoolboy watching his teacher circle mistakes with a red pen.

"You are ready." Macario said.

"What about the missing flats?"

"I will look. If they are just by the road, we will not worry. We get them later. Only problem is people that steal them."

"Cannery flats?"

"*Sí.* To use in their work places—you know, for the nails and screws and bolts. You go back to the farm. I make sure there is no *problema.*"

"Thanks, Macario. Sorry about the hassle."

"Is okay." Macario smiled. "Now, you are real truck driver."

Jeff no longer felt like puking all over the road. He climbed back in the cab. "Oh, I almost forgot," he called to Macario, "we found five flats with rocks and dirt in the bottom."

Macario opened the GMC door and paused on the running board. "Ah, *bandidos.* Bad luck for the Hamptons but more bad luck for these persons." He nodded good-bye.

Pulling onto the county road, Jeff squinted through the dusty windshield. Late afternoon sun beat straight into the cab. The black electrical tape coating the steering wheel had turned sticky, and the metal dashboard radiated heat. Jeff flipped a silver latch and pushed open the small winged window, sending a rush of warm dry air across his face.

He shifted gears and gazed at the deserted road. In his Bronco, he would have been tearing toward the Coast Range. Now, it felt okay to be lumbering along at forty-five in the loaded flatbed.

"WNWP836—unit three to unit ten."

Jeff snatched the radio on the seat. Steering with one hand, he pushed the speaker lever. "Unit ten—go ahead."

"*Hola.* I see the flats. Is no *problema.* They are most in the ditch. I will pick up some on the way back. Maybe, if Mr. Hampton goes to town, he picks up some, too. I will tell him."

"No, wait." Jeff spoke carefully into the radio. "I'll get them on my way home tonight."

"*Está bien.* Unit three clear."

"Thanks a lot, Macario. Unit ten clear." Jeff set the radio down and fixed his eyes on the hazy blue Coast Range. "Think you could spare a little rain? In Mexico? Over *Río* something or other?"

Libby, Alexa, Mrs. Hampton, and Ethel were sitting in a circle next to the scales when Jeff returned to the field. A woman and two small children were u-picking in the Bentons. He could hear country music coming from Mrs. Hampton's pickup.

"Playing poker?" he asked.

"No, silly," said Libby. "We're adding up tickets. Here, have some." She held out a bunch of wrinkled, smudged picker tickets. "See. Wherever it's punched, add the numbers across and write it at the end. Put the total in the corner and circle it."

"I think some of the numbers are wrong," Jeff said.

"Whatdaya mean?" Libby looked puzzled.

"The lady taking the samples found five flats with rocks and dirt on the bottom."

Mrs. Hampton shook her head and set her tickets in a shoe box.

"Rats," said Ethel. She crossed her arms under her full chest.

"Coke?" Alexa asked Jeff.

"Sure."

"Catch." She tossed him a can.

"I'll bet that jerk Danny did it," said Libby.

"And just how would he do it when he's been fired?" quizzed Alexa, pointing 'think' to her temple.

"I don't know, smarty," Libby huffed, "but at least I'm trying to figure it out."

"Thank you, Libby," said Mrs. Hampton. "This is a hard one." She sighed and looked at Jeff. "Did we get docked?"

"No, but we need to find out who's doing it." He pulled the weight slip from his back pocket. "16,432 pounds."

"That's good," she said, taking the paper.

"How was your trip?" asked Alexa.

"Oh, all right—I guess." He grabbed several flats and set them on the ground.

They worked in silence, occasionally comparing totals or recalling minor catastrophes of the day. "I couldn't believe this one guy." Ethel's eyes narrowed. "The nerve. He waltzes out here middle of the morning. Says he's been sent from the employment office. Hands me his little white card to sign. We do all the paperwork. I give him a row, and a half hour later he says he has to go into town for cigarettes. I never see him again. A complete waste of my time."

"That's as bad as the brain surgeon," said Alexa. Everyone laughed.

"I'm missing something here," said Jeff.

"It's a good one." Libby bit into a Milky Way.

Alexa set her calculator in her lap. "A few years ago, Dad called the state employment office to see if we could get some people out here to pick. This lady told him they didn't have any qualified berry pickers. He told her he'd be happy to teach anyone the fine art of berry picking. She said that people didn't have to pick if it wasn't their chosen line of work."

"I'll bet your dad loved that," Jeff said.

"He told her, 'You mean, if you have a brain surgeon collecting unemployment, he can't come out and pick my crop that's rotting in the field?' Then she said, 'I'll have you know, mister, there are no unemployed brain surgeons in our county.'"

They all laughed again.

Alexa stretched. "I'm going swimming."

"Me, too," said Libby, jumping up.

"Thanks for your help, Jeff." Mrs. Hampton gathered the calculators and pencils.

"No problem."

"See you all in the morning," said Ethel. "Don't you worry about that berry cheat, Jeff. We'll catch him."

He nodded.

With the field to himself, he unloaded empty flats and positioned the Ford for the next day. Walking around to the rear of the truck, he leaned back against the bed, pulled his T-shirt out from his jeans and wiped his face. Everything was so still. Just the faint droning of the pumps, and the hum of some insect. A bird called from its nest in the cattails. Jeff filled his lungs with the early evening air and closed his eyes for a moment.

Walking back to his Bronco, he heard shrieks of laughter coming from across the lake. Squinting, he could see Libby splashing water next to the dock. He recognized Alexa's blond hair as she moved to the dock's edge, bent to a racing dive, and flung herself out over the water. She pierced the surface with a clean entry and resurfaced a few seconds later, her arms moving in a strong freestyle. She swam gracefully toward the middle of the lake, turning her head ever so slightly with each stroke.

Jeff unlocked his car door and rolled down the window. He watched again as Alexa disappeared behind a wooden raft, then pulled herself up. Tilting her head to one side, she squeezed water from her hair. She waved to Libby, then stretched out on the sun-baked boards.

Chapter 11

WHEN JEFF ARRIVED AT THE FIELD the next morning, his Bronco was stuffed with yellow cannery flats.

He'd driven home slowly the night before, inspecting ditches and stopping in driveways to gather orphaned crates. Several had bounced clear across the road, the remains of two smashings scattered on the pavement.

"I wonder where you found these," Alexa said as he hauled an armful to the empty stacks.

"Around."

She smiled. "We heard you and Macario on the radio."

Jeff groaned. "So your dad knows."

"He knows everything." She walked back to his car with him.

"I'll bet he does." Jeff filled her outstretched arms with the sorry looking flats. "Some of these are dead."

"Roadkill?"

Jeff rolled his eyes. "That's bad."

Mrs. Hampton called them to the scales. Libby sat on Ethel's folding chair, yawning. Ethel leaned next to the truck, eating a granola bar.

"Jake had an idea about the rocks," Mrs. Hampton said. "If the picker doing this isn't careful, the flats will obviously weigh more than they should. Alexa, Libby, keep an eye on the scales today. See if anything looks unusual. Or," she nodded to Jeff, "feels especially heavy."

Libby put her hands to her forehead. "I seeee something," she said in a wavering voice. "He's short and he's wearing an orange and black baseball hat with a chain saw on it. Ohhhh, let me look closer, he's wearing a jean jacket with nothing under it, just his bare belly hanging out."

"Libby, what are you saying?" asked Mrs. Hampton.

"I remember this one guy's flats weighing more yesterday. He always wears that dirty jean jacket—even when it's really hot. You'd think he'd roast."

"I know who you're talking about," said Ethel.

"I'm not really sure," Libby said, hesitating. "There were a lot of people in line and I was hurrying awful fast."

"He probably took his flats to Libby because she gets flustered so easy," said Alexa.

"Nah-uh. Just wait, Alexa, I'll catch him, then you'll see."

It wasn't until the lunchtime rush that jean-jacket guy came out of the field. Jeff saw him from the corner of his eye, pushing a wheelie stacked with five or six flats. He got in Libby's line. Jeff glanced around the field. Mrs. Hampton was walking casually to her pickup. Ethel moved toward the scale.

Macario pulled into the field with the GMC, parking along the south edge.

"Maybe we play soccer for lunch," he said to Jeff as he reached the Ford. He held a ball in one hand.

Jeff jumped off the truck. "Or, maybe," he said quietly, "we catch a *bandido* for lunch."

Macario's brown eyes turned serious. "*¿Sí?*"

Jeff nodded. "It might be that guy in the jean jacket in Libby's line." Jeff kept his back to the scales.

Macario stole a glance around Jeff's shoulder.

"Do you know him?" Jeff asked.

"No." Macario shook his head, frowning. "You are surprised? Because he is Mexican does not mean that I know him."

"I just thought since you've worked here a long time you might know him, that's all," Jeff tried to explain.

"Yes, I understand," said Macario. "I just sometimes am tired of the American idea that *all* Mexicans look the same and talk the same or are lazy or good workers. We are all different peoples."

"You're right, Macario, you are all different." Jeff paused. "Especially you."

"*Cómico.*"

"Huh?"

"You are comedian."

Jeff returned to the weigh station just as Jean-Jacket set two flats on Libby's scale.

Libby looked wide-eyed as Jeff began sorting through the top flat.

"*¡Aye!*" protested the man.

"Checking for rot." Jeff dipped into the berries but couldn't find anything suspicious. Nothing.

Libby had turned pale. She examined Jean Jacket's ticket. "Benito Hernández-Pech. Thirty-eight pounds," she said weakly.

Jeff's stomach knotted. He yanked the flats off Libby's scale.

"Check the bottom flat," whispered Alexa. "Old trick."

Jeff placed the flats on the ground and set the top one

aside. He dug into the bottom flat and practically gagged. He looked up. A number of pickers had crowded around by now, everyone staring at the flat.

"What did you find, Jeff?" Mr. Hampton pushed through to the scale.

"This guy isn't quite sure what a strawberry looks like," said Jeff, nodding at Benito and tossing more berries aside. A thick layer of gravel lined the flat.

"Let's check your other flats," said Mr. Hampton, turning to Benito.

He started to object, but Mr. Hampton bent down and quickly searched each crate. "Three more." He stood up and faced Benito. "You are stealing from us."

"*No comprendo inglés.*"

Mr. Hampton eyed him.

Benito shook his head.

Mr. Hampton spoke in Spanish. His words were as clear as the vein in his neck.

"Tell him there's no pay for these flats with the rocks, and I'll mail his check tomorrow." Mrs. Hampton made a note on her clipboard.

This time the words flew from Mr. Hampton's mouth. His hands waved and jabbed at the air, then landed on his hips with the last word.

Benito turned sharply, muttered under his breath, and pushed past the silent crowd.

Chapter 12

ONE WEEK. IT'D BEEN ONE FULL WEEK since he'd started. Jeff paused at the end of his driveway and stared at a long, pink cloud stretching across sleepy Salem. Far across the Willamette Valley, guarding the eastern horizon, stood Mt. Hood in military dress blues. He turned off his radio and rolled down the window. Cool fresh air poured into the car. A bird broke the silence. A moment later, another bird answered, and their conversation began.

He drove down through the West Salem hills and entered the deserted strip of shopping malls and fast-food restaurants. Bright signs announced real estate, insurance, pizza, and burgers. Traffic signals lit empty intersections.

A week, he mused as he passed a final string of gas stations and car washes. It felt like a month. Up at 4:15. In the car at 4:45. To the field by 5:15. Lift, load, stack. Lunch break. Sometimes. Lift, load, stack, hot sun, weigh fruit, punch tickets, rope down. Drive to the cannery. Drive back from the cannery. He'd learned not to count on being done at any particular time. There was always an outhouse to move or water tank to refill. Tickets to add up. Empties to unload.

One evening, when a sharp pain grabbed his stomach, he realized he hadn't eaten all day. It was even difficult to find time to pee. He still hesitated each time he opened the blue Top Pots door, wishing he could just take a leak behind the truck.

All this for a little red berry. Amazing. Give it some sun and water and, bingo—berserk berries. Thousands of them, exploding from tiny green to giant red. Ordering your life around. With the burst of berries came the swarm of pickers. Sometimes there were so many people they had to double up, a situation most did not like except the young American kids who were always whining for someone to "help finish my row."

Macario would arrive about an hour after picking had started. He'd survey the crew and wander the field. "I see how much *fruta* we have," he explained to Jeff. Once, when the Ford was just two-thirds full, he started tying it down. "We have three loads today. I will go now."

Bethel Road began to look the same no matter which direction Jeff drove. He knew time was passing as he watched certain fields. One day they'd be filled with tall, bending grass. Then they'd be mowed and lined with evenly spaced windrows. Next came the bales, looking like tightly wrapped packages. Driving home one evening, he slowed to watch a large machine race around the field, scooping up bales and cramming them backward into a huge holding pen. With a full load, the machine scurried over to a long wall of neatly stacked bales and pushed out its giant bundle. It reminded him of a river-bottom bug, darting about the rocky floor, hunting wildly for food.

Jeff found himself searching each morning for the speckled hawk. He knew just how close he could get before the bird would drop from its perch with the form of a championship diver, gray and brown wings spread wide, soft white belly bared to the earth. Sometimes, when it soared majestically across the wheat fields, Jeff tried to imagine what it would be like to swoop and dip and glide.

A week didn't seem long enough to work out the kinks, he thought now as he passed the hawk's territory, but the aches and pains had disappeared, and he felt stronger. He could tell when he lifted two heavy flats from the scales, hauled them to the truck, hoisted them onto the bed, pulled himself up, and stacked them without as much effort. Plus, he'd been doing all those crazy soccer drills, and now Macario had Jeff practicing while holding a loaded flat. Sometimes at lunch they'd kick the ball around, Macario shouting at Jeff to stay on his toes, Alexa and Libby laughing and clapping.

Without his mom's reminder, Jeff would have forgotten the original time line. Just that morning in the hallway, she had said, "Two more weeks, and you should have that pump paid off. If not, we'll take care of the rest. We've got to get you back on the courts—the college recruiters will be showing up soon."

"Oh," she had said, pausing at the bathroom door, "Debbie called last night. You were already in bed. I tried to explain how tired you were and that this shouldn't last much longer."

His mom was right about being tired. When he did manage to talk to Debbie, he could barely keep up his end of this conversation. "Jeff, are you listening to me?" she'd ask impatiently after a long silence.

"Oh, yeah, hi."

"Jeffery. Wake up. Aaron's having everyone over tomorrow. Let's go."

He'd forgotten Aaron's party after a tedious delay at the cannery. Debbie went without him.

★　★　★

As Jeff passed the grain tanks, something in the road caught his eye. He stopped and squinted back at the closest tank. Same old fuzzy black spray paint.

Stepping from the Bronco, he knelt down and examined the gravel. Gun shells—.22s—all over the place. He jogged to the tanks. Sure enough. Bullet holes splattered across the back of the first and second tanks.

"What's going on around here?" he asked Alexa as soon as he arrived at the field.

"What do you mean?"

"The tanks."

"We still don't know who painted them," she said, "but that was just last week."

"I'm not talking about the paint. I'm talking about these." He held the small brass bullet shells flat in the palm of his hand. "The tanks have been shot up."

Alexa stared.

"Didn't you see them?"

"No . . . I guess we were talking about today's pick and . . . I . . . I don't know. We just drove right by." She stopped talking, then took a deep breath and jammed her teeth together. Jeff could see her cheekbones flexing beneath her skin. "Those . . . those . . . bastards."

"Has your dad seen it?"

She shook her head. "He went straight to the computer this morning."

Alexa showed the cartridges to her mother. When Mrs. Hampton radioed the news to Mr. Hampton, he growled back, "I don't have time for this!"

At lunch that day, Alexa sat in the shade of the empty flats. As Jeff walked by, she stuck out her foot. He stumbled and regained his balance.

"Goll, Alexa," said Libby from the flatbed. "What a dork. You want someone to trip *you*?"

"Yeah, Alexa," Jeff mimicked Libby, "that wasn't very nice." He winked at Libby.

Jeff tapped his foot on the ground next to Alexa. "This seat taken?"

"Nope."

"But you always sit up here." Libby frowned.

"I'll be back," Jeff told her.

"Try this." Alexa handed him a glass bottle.

He took a sip and gagged. Strawberry something. "How can you drink strawberry *anything*?"

"You big baby." Alexa grabbed the bottle but he wouldn't let go. She used both hands, but still couldn't pry it loose. Now juice spurted out. "Ack." Alexa laughed. "It's in my hair."

"Where it belongs," said Jeff. "Strawberry shampoo."

"There's a van coming in," said Libby, peering down the road.

"U-pickers?" Jeff asked.

Alexa shrugged.

"I know," said Libby, grinning. "What's today?"

"Thursday," Jeff answered.

"What else?"

Alexa stood up and watched as the van stopped at the crossroad. A woman walked to the back, opened the door, and pulled out a flower arrangement.

"From your boyfriend?" teased Libby.

Jeff looked curiously at Alexa. She wouldn't make eye contact.

"From Corey or Miguel?" Libby spoke more to Jeff than Alexa.

"Lay off," Alexa shot back.

"Happy birthday, sweetheart," said Mrs. Hampton.

"Thanks, Mom."

Jeff almost laughed. There stood Alexa, dirt smeared across her nose, berry stains on her faded jeans, juice in her hair, holding this beautiful bouquet of tulips and daisies. Somehow, he couldn't see Debbie in the same situation.

Alexa curtsied to the group saying, "Thank you, thank you." She made a table of empty flats next to her scale and placed the arrangement in the center.

Mr. Hampton showed up next. He got out of his pick-up, awkwardly balancing a cardboard bakery box. "For the birthday girl," he said, kissing Alexa on the cheek. "And, in honor of your day, I reported the grain tank shooting to the sheriff's office."

"Thanks, Dad, but I was hoping for a pickup."

"Dream on," said Libby.

★　★　★

Cattails rustled as a gust of wind crossed the lake. Jeff shivered and glanced at the gray clouds covering the sun.

"Where'd they come from?" He bent down from the GMC, handing Macario an armload of empty flats.

"*No sé.* The man on the radio, he says it rains tomorrow."

"All right. A day off."

Macario grinned. "You are *muy loco.*"

"What?"

"Crazy—you are very crazy—we work in the sun and the rain."

A day off. He could have practiced in the morning

and spent time with Debbie. Maybe a drive and dinner at the beach.

"You are very quiet," said Macario. "Did you have *problemas* today at the cannery?"

"Nah." The cannery trips had become routine now, and even though Venancio's foot was better, Mr. Hampton had decided to keep Jeff driving. Venancio was needed on some big irrigation project, and Mr. Hampton had even praised Jeff, saying he was doing a 'surprisingly good job.'

Macario picked up a rope and began coiling it.

Jeff picked up another one. "I just don't have any time these days."

"The girlfriend?"

"She gets nervous if we don't see each other a lot."

"Is she to be your wife?"

Jeff's eyebrows shot up. "I'm not ready to get married."

"Maybe she is?" Macario smiled.

"No, no. She just wants to go steady."

"Steady?"

"It's when you only date one person."

Macario concentrated on tying a knot. "I know about steady. When I am sixteen years old, I like Teresa. She is fourteen. I know her before that—we live on the same ranch—but all at once I like her. I go to see her, but her father is very angry. He says no dating. No even speak to each other. One time we are together at the well, and we talk. Her father, he whipped her."

"You're kidding."

Macario shook his head. "But we see each other again behind a tree near her *casa*. Teresa's *mamá* catches us and says the father will whip her again. I say 'No—if he does this, then we run away.'"

"Did you?"

"No. Her *mamá* must say something to the father. He say we can talk, but just at their house."

Macario loaded the ropes inside the truck cab and glanced at the sky. "Maybe the rain comes tonight."

"So, Macario, you eventually got to marry Teresa, right?"

"Oh, *sí*. A few years later, *mi papá* he asks the *Padre* of the church to go and speak to Teresa's father. Her *papá* say we must think about it for six months and not to see each other."

"Six months? What a rip." Jeff shook his head. "He'd never get away with that here."

Macario smiled. "After the six months, we say we still want to marry and we find a day for the wedding."

The wind knocked an empty flat to the ground and Jeff set it back on the stack. "Big party?"

"Oh, *sí*. The weddings, they are competition in Mexico. Who has the biggest, you know?" Macario gave a sheepish grin.

Jeff realized that, for the first time, Macario was actually poking fun at his own people.

"You invite all your friends?" Jeff asked.

"No invitations. Just talk to people, they tell others. Even peoples we don't know come."

"Really?"

"Is okay. Is custom. We say '*un invitado, invita a diez*'."

"Which means?"

"One guest invites ten."

"Geezus, break the bank."

Macario nodded. "We kill a pig. There are many foods. The women, even Teresa, they start cooking at four in the morning."

"Then you party?"

"No,no. The wedding mass is first. Then the *fiesta*—food, *música*, dancing."

"I don't suppose Teresa's father let you take her away for a honeymoon."

"The *luna de miel*. We go one week to Guadalajara." Macario's smile faded. "Is *maravilloso*." The word lingered and Jeff discovered longing.

Chapter
13

THE NEXT MORNING A DARK CEILING hung low across the valley. Thick, dingy clouds spilled over the Coast Range and crept down the foothills. Smoky wisps of fog twisted up from forested canyons and reached to touch the sagging sky.

Only a few cars parked alongside the field. No children ran about, laughing and chasing each other. Workers sat crammed in their cars. Someone blew cigarette smoke out a half-opened window. One man leaning against his car nodded to Jeff, then said something.

"What?" Jeff rolled down his window.

"*Panza de burra.*"

Something about a burro. He'd have to ask Macario. This language business, Jeff had decided, was sort of like a quiz show. Pick out the words you do know, guess at the ones that sound familiar, and come up with the winning sentence. Actually, a lot of Spanish words came pretty close to the English versions. Like car and *carro*, plant and *planta*, telephone and *teléfono*. If all else failed, he sometimes added an *o* or *a* to the end and hoped it worked.

Jeff wasn't sure if Macario's Spanish lessons were due to generosity or amusement. The latest laugh came when Jeff mispronounced *papá* and called his father a potato.

Macario often warned, "*Más bajo.* Your loud voice will not make me understand."

Jeff occasionally returned the lessons with a few English tips. One evening, as he unloaded the Ford, he kept looking down Bethel Road for Macario and the GMC. Had Macario lost a stack of empties? Run out of gas? Broken down? At last, the truck lumbered into the field, and when Macario hopped out of the cab, Jeff asked, "*¿Problemas?*"

"No. The constitution makes me late."

What did the Constitution have to do with driving? Jeff quickly traced the route in his mind, then started to laugh. "You mean the construction. The road work in West Salem."

Macario smiled. "Ah, *sí*, the construction. Most usually, I have not the difficulty with the words, but I have trouble building the sentences."

★　★　★

By seven-thirty that morning, only half the rows in section four had been taken.

"Where is everyone?" asked Jeff.

"The Mexican women probably stayed home with their children." Alexa checked the sky. "And the locals— well, we might get a few diehards, but most of them are fair-weather pickers."

"What about Libby?"

"She's at the house—coming down with something."

"I thought that kid was bulletproof."

A drop of rain hit Alexa's face. Another splashed off

her rubber boots. She scowled and snapped up her yellow slicker. "Where's your rain gear?"

"Home." Jeff zipped his sweatshirt.

"Nice going."

Ethel hurried out of a row. "Where are the garbage sacks?"

"In Mom's pickup."

Laughing and pointed at each other, the pickers poked their heads and arms through the plastic. Soon the field was dotted with turtle-shaped mounds rummaging around in the berry plants.

Suddenly the rain cranked into high gear, pounding the plants and ground and slap-smacking against the plastic.

"Take a break!" yelled Mrs. Hampton. She led the way across the field to the large oak tree. Black bundles followed, hopping over rows and slipping in the muddy aisles.

Alexa made a beeline for the truck cab. "In here!" she shouted to Jeff.

He jumped off the flatbed, lost his balance on the wet dirt, and fell on his rear. Rain dribbled off his hair and down his back as he got up and stumbled to the cab door.

"Whew," he said, climbing in the driver's side and slamming the door. Alexa had taken off her jacket and was shaking her hair.

Jeff wiped his muddy hands on his jeans. "Now what?"

"We'll see what the rain's going to do. If it stops, or even slows down, we'll keep picking. Otherwise, that's it for the day."

Jeff leaned back against the seat and watched the raindrops splash onto the windshield. They clung briefly to the glass before sliding down like oval-headed pollywogs, their long, skinny tails wagging and gathering stray droplets.

The cab reverberated with the pelting of rain against the roof. A damp, musty smell filled the cramped compartment, and the heavy odor of warm bodies worked its way through water-soaked clothes and hair.

Alexa's eyes were closed, her lashes still wet. Her hair was pulled back into a ponytail, revealing a small circle of brown skin below her left earlobe. Jeff hadn't noticed the earrings until now—tiny gold seashells. She didn't wear makeup, but her cheeks were the flushed red of someone who worked outdoors a lot.

She opened her eyes. Jeff quickly looked at the steering wheel and began running a hand around its taped rim.

"It seems like lately . . . " Alexa started and then stopped.

"What?"

"Um." She cleared her throat. "You're happier these days. Well, maybe not happier, just not so grouchy."

Jeff fiddled with a loose piece of black electrical tape. "You've seemed happier, too," he said. That sounded dumb. The words echoed in the cab and whirled in his head: "Happier, happier."

"So, the job's okay?" She pulled off her rubber boots and put her feet up on the dash.

"It's not bad. At least I'm outside."

"Is our farm what you expected?" She settled back against the seat.

"I don't know what I expected." Jeff wiped the fogged windshield with his shirtsleeve. "Maybe some animals."

"Chickens, pigs and cows, right? Old MacDonald had a farm?" Alexa's mouth turned up at the corners.

"Yeah, right. E-I-E-I-O." He relaxed his arm across the back of the seat, his fingers brushing against her hair.

"Sorry to disappoint you. All we've got are two horses, one dog and three barn cats."

"That's it—the barn." Jeff tugged at her hair. "Barns are supposed to be red. Yours is white."

Alexa laughed. "And all barns have a silo."

"So where's yours?" He peered out the window.

"You're hopeless," She kicked his leg. "Go back to the city where you belong," she said, shivering.

"You cold? Want me to warm up the truck?" Jeff reached for the key.

"That's okay. The rain's stopping. We'll probably start up in a few minutes."

Jeff studied the windshield. The pollywogs clung to their resting places, merging now with other droplets. The black bags were straggling back to the field, stepping gingerly over the soggy rows.

"This will be a major mess." Alexa pulled on her boots and rain jacket. "Your feet are going to feel like concrete blocks."

★ ★ ★

By early afternoon, the truck was a sheet of slippery brown goo, and Jeff virtually tiptoed across the wooden boards. When Macario arrived, he looked at the sky and shook his head. *Panza de burra.*

"That's the second time today," Jeff said. "What is it?"

"'Belly of the burro.'" Macario scooped his hand through the air. "Is low, heavy. It means the rain, it is close. There is no edge to the sky."

"Darn rain," Mrs. Hampton said wearily when she called it a day. "I'd hoped to finish section four." She poured a cup of coffee from her thermos and took a sip.

"I hate to do this to you, Jeff, but we're going to need everybody out here tomorrow. If there's any way you can miss your tennis tournament, I'd really appreciate it."

Jeff felt his body numb. They'd discussed the Eugene tournament yesterday. The plan was to finish section four and have the weekend off again.

"I'm getting nervous," she said. "We've got rot out here now. We can't possibly wait until Monday. And," she sighed, "the Totems are crying for a third pick."

Before Jeff could respond, she added, "That's okay. You don't have to tell me now. Just show up if you can."

★   ★   ★

Jeff lay awake in bed that night, staring at the faint reflection from his trophies.

He crossed his arms beneath his head and closed his eyes. So what's it gonna be? Tennis? Or sloppy, muddy, rotten berries? Just show up *if you can*, she had said. No pressure.

But the more he tried to reassure himself, the harder his heart pounded. Stop! This is not a big deal! Just play the tournament and show up earlier Monday morning.

He rolled over and smothered his face in his pillow. Now he could feel his heart beating against the mattress.

"Damn!" he said out loud, sitting up and tossing off his sheet and blanket. He switched on a light, squinted, and grabbed the phone. He punched at the numbers and waited impatiently for a voice.

Finally, "Hel-lo."

"Jason, this is Jeff."

"Geezuz, man . . . What are you doing? . . . You partying?"

"Listen, Jason—I can't play tomorrow. You gotta get a sub, okay?"

"What? Are you crazy, man? *You* listen. We need this win tomorrow and you need to watch your ranking. Have you forgotten? The Invitational and Sam Nelson are only two weeks away."

"Who says I'll end up with Nelson? I could bomb out in the first round."

"Exactly, stupid. That's why you've got to be in Eugene."

"I've gotta be at the farm tomorrow. The Hampton's could lose their crop."

Chapter 14

THE WEIGHT OF LAST NIGHT'S DECISION held Jeff in bed the next morning. He wistfully imagined wearing warm-ups and tying his Nike Flares. Instead, he pulled on thick socks and rubber boots and tossed his rain jacket in the back seat of his Bronco.

He told himself he had a right to be angry. But, as he left town and headed toward the Coast Range, the anger wouldn't come. He passed Martha's without stopping and realized he was anxious to get the berries picked before they turned to mush.

Jeff's hawk wasn't perched on its usual spot. He surveyed a soggy field of baled alfalfa. *Mala suerte*, he thought. Some farmer was surely cursing the change in weather. Wet hay meant a lower price, no matter how much it dried out.

Dodging mud puddles and soft spots, he crested a small hill and came upon a mass of hawks filling the sky, soaring in a spiral figure eight. There had to be twenty-five or thirty of them. He tried to count but lost track as his eyes moved up the formation. There they were, the entire sky open to them, and no little blackbirds dive-bombing, poking and pecking. It was as if some lead hawk had called out the dance and the others followed in perfect sync, neatly spaced, floating upward without a single beat of their wings.   Jeff following their effortless sweep up and glide down, up again, higher this time, and back down. He tried to find his hawk, but it was impossible. Two birds suddenly broke from the top of the spiral. They soared a bit higher, then swept out across a freshly cut field.

★　★　★

With the berry field sloppy wet, Jeff parked along the gravel road. He grabbed his jacket and walked past the string of cars.

A rich aroma touched the cool air. Jeff's stomach growled. He could see a man and woman standing beside a small propane stove, set in the gravel next to their car. The woman bent to stir something in a cast iron frying pan. The man smiled as Jeff got closer. "*Buenos días,*"said the man.

"*Buenos días,*" Jeff answered. He recognized the couple. They picked every day, and they always cooked from this little stove at lunch. The man's front tooth was chipped and the skin around his mouth pulled tight into deep wrinkles.

The woman had a woolen scarf on her head and two button-up sweaters over her blouse. She wore tennis shoes with no socks. "*¿Quieres?*" she asked, pointing to the dark, thick, bean mixture in the pan.

Jeff was about to decline, but he'd left the house that morning without breakfast. He nodded. "*Gracias.*"

The woman's face beamed. She quickly reached for a small basket on the hood of the car and carefully pulled back the edge of a dishtowel. Inside was a stack of corn tortillas. She urged him to take one.

He was about to grab the top tortilla, when she shook her head and pointed down the pile. *"Más caliente."*

Using both hands, Jeff pulled out a middle tortilla. It was warm and pliable.

The woman stirred the beans, then lifted a heaping spoonful. Jeff moved his tortilla to catch the food. Now what? he wondered. He'd eaten his share of Taco Bell burritos, but they always came pre-rolled.

The man snatched the top tortilla and helped himself to the beans. Then he folded one edge over about an inch and began rolling an adjoining side across the filling like he was taking up a piece of carpet. He looked at Jeff, raised his eyebrows, then took a bite.

Jeff followed the directions, hoping nothing would fall out. A spicy tang swept through his mouth, but the spice didn't overwhelm the other flavors. It was good. Very good. Or maybe food just tasted better alongside a gravel road on a cold, wet morning.

The man offered Jeff an orange drink from a mayonnaise jar. Jeff shook his head. When he finished his last bite, he wiped his mouth on the back of his hand.

"¿Otra?" the woman asked eagerly, and the man reached for the basket.

"No, thank you. It was great, though." Jeff could hear himself beginning to shout. He tried to lower his voice. "Thanks a lot. *Gracias.*"

"De nada," said the man, almost bowing. The woman smiled broadly. *"Adiós."*

Jeff gave a slight wave, turned, and moved briskly between cars, through the ditch, and down the closest row.

"Over here," Mrs. Hampton called. She was squatting

next to a row behind the truck. Mr. Hampton knelt opposite her and raised his hand as Jeff approached.

"Thanks for coming," said Mrs. Hampton. "Sorry about your tournament."

"That's okay."

"We're all picking for now," she said. "You can start on Ethel's row and work toward her."

Jeff grabbed an empty flat and stepped across the drenched plants.

"¡Hola!" Macario called from his row. His brothers, Jerónimo and Santiago, looked up and smiled.

"Hi, Jeff!" Libby hollered from a few rows away.

"I thought you were sick." He dropped his flat on the ground and bent over.

"I was." She bit into a berry. "But Dad says I'm well enough to pick."

Alexa stood and stretched. "Bum deal about your tennis."

"Yeah. Oh, well." He shrugged and began searching through a plant. There wasn't as much rot as he'd expected. More disgusting was the tiny, gray slug chewing away the backside of a perfectly good berry. Especially disgusting when the slug slimed against his hand.

Steam began rising from the field as the sun slipped between ragged clouds. Jeff settled into a rhythm, moving through the leaves, picking and dumping. This was probably the best time of the day, he thought. Not too cold or too hot. Pickers weren't tired yet, or sore, or hungry. No one was waiting at the scales or asking to u-pick. A few birds chattered from their nests in the cattails. Several pickers began singing a low song.

Jeff stood up and pulled off his sweatshirt. *Whack!* A splash of red marked the shoulder of his white T-shirt and a good-sized berry lay on the ground next to his feet.

"Hey!" He looked quickly around the field. Alexa's head shot down, but Jeff could see her grin.

"She can't get away with that," Mr. Hampton said mischievously.

Jeff nodded and picked three squishy, furry berries. Casually, he stepped over the rows.

"Oh, no you don't!" Alexa tried to run, but Jeff caught her arm and crammed the berries down her back.

"Aaack!" She snatched a berry from the closest bush and hurled it at him. "You!" she yelled.

He grabbed two more and smashed them in her hair.

"Get her!" shouted Libby.

Alexa went for her flat, scooping a handful. Jeff jumped back and hopped across the rows. Pickers sat up, clapping and whooping as he returned to his spot.

"I'm not done with you!" Alexa called.

"You started it!"

★ ★ ★

Jeff opened his cooler and studied the contents. He shut the lid.

"Aren't you going to eat?" asked Libby.

"I'm not hungry."

"How come?" asked Alexa.

"A lady and her husband fed me this morning." He pointed to the road. "A fantastic Mexican breakfast."

"Must be Carmen and Enrique Gómez," said Alexa. She popped a green grape into her mouth.

"How do you know?" asked Jeff.

"Can we tell him?" Alexa asked her dad.

"I suppose," said Mr. Hampton. "Carmen and Enrique came to our house after the first day of picking. They asked if they could sleep in their car someplace on our farm. I said they could. The next night they asked again and I told them 'no,' that I could get in trouble. They pleaded." Mr. Hampton paused a moment. "I said, 'The answer's no but I won't be looking very hard.'"

"And," blurted Libby, "Dad told them they had to be parked on Bethel Road every morning before any pickers got here."

"They were probably running late today," said Alexa.

"Where do they stay?" asked Jeff and immediately felt he'd asked too much.

Alexa pointed behind the strawberry field to a clump of oak trees.

"*Hola.*" Macario joined the group. He was carving an apple with his pocketknife and offered a piece to Jeff.

"No, thanks."

"Jeff says he had a real Mexican breakfast this morning," announced Libby.

"What is that?" Macario asked.

"A tortilla with this great bean stuff in it," Jeff told him.

Macario smiled. "Do you think all Mexican food is tortillas and beans?" He chewed a piece of apple.

Jeff shrugged.

"Is all American food hot dogs and hamburgers?"

"No."

"In Mexico, we eat many the same things you do. Fish, beefsteak, chicken, pig, goat."

"Wrong on the goat, Macario."

"Oh, that is for *especial* occasion. We slaughter a goat if you come to Mexico to visit *mi familia.*"

"So what did you have for lunch today?" asked Jeff.

Macario blushed. "Tortillas and beans."

Jeff pointed at Macario and everyone laughed.

★　★　★

After lunch another Hampton employee came to pick. As the guy drove in on a four-wheeler, Jeff realized there were probably a number of full-time workers he had never met. He'd seen them from a distance moving pipe, driving tractors, fixing broken sprinklers, but their paths had never crossed.

Jeff couldn't help but stare. This man looked as stout and tough as a pit bull. His black sweatshirt hugged tight across his broad chest and he wore black Wranglers that also fit snug around his thick thighs. His black baseball hat read "MidLane Truck Repair," and a red, white, and blue Harley-Davidson scarf hung from the back of the hat, shading his neck.

Macario called from the flatbed, then rattled something in Spanish, pointing to the field. The guy nodded and turned to go, slipping on his dark sunglasses with a gloved hand. The glove had all the fingers chopped off at the mid-knuckle.

"*Un momento*," Macario said, signaling him to come closer. "This is Jeff McKenzie."

"Nice to meet you," said Jeff, handing a couple of flats up to Macario.

"This is Casimiro Acosta-Solis," introduced Macario.

Casimiro grinned, flashing a silver tooth. He extended his hand. Jeff gripped the rough glove and found himself fumbling as Casimiro moved into the second handshake. "*El gusto es mío*," said Casimiro seriously.

Jeff nodded and tried not to smile at the faded red Santa Claus stretching across Casimiro's sweatshirt.

Casimiro grinned again. The Mexican workers, Jeff had noticed, did a lot of this grinning and smiling, and he'd decided it was their way of responding when they didn't understand someone. It also seemed to be their technique to diffuse confrontation. He'd seen it numerous times as Alexa warned or scolded about heavy flats or too many stems, or rot. They'd nod and smile, assuring her it would never happen again.

"*Adiós*," said Casimiro, breaking the awkward silence.

"*Adiós*," Jeff and Macario said in unison.

Casimiro wandered into the field with a tall stack of empty flats balanced on his shoulder.

"What's *el gusto* something or other?" Jeff asked Macario. "Everyone says it when I meet them."

Macario walked to the edge of the flatbed and knelt down. "The first person, he say, '*Mucho gusto*'—pleased to meet you. Then the other person say back, '*El gusto es mió*'—the pleasure is mine."

"You didn't say it when I first met you."

"You didn't say 'pleased to meet you.'"

★   ★   ★

That afternoon, instead of the normal slowdown, there seemed to be an air of determination. The field was quiet as pickers pushed to finish their rows. As always, they picked from the far end of the field toward the crossroad so now there was a string of people closing in on the truck.

Alexa and Libby were busy weighing. Jeff shuttled flats to the truck. Macario stacked. Only one load today, but a pretty full one.

"Oh, yuck!" Libby suddenly cried out. "He just picked an earwig off a berry and he ate it!" Her face wrinkled in disgust as she pointed to the man standing at her scales. He grinned.

"Earwigs?" Jeff questioned Macario.

"You think, now, all Mexicans eat earwigs, *¿sí?* Do all Americans eat grasshoppers?"

Jeff rolled his eyes. "Only chocolate-covered ones."

He returned to Alexa's scale and hoisted the flats from the metal platform. "Thanks," she said, and he felt her voice follow him as he moved to the truck. He set the load on the muddy flatbed and glanced back. She was busily reading the needle on her scale.

Carmen Gómez walked out of her row carrying two flats.

"Look out!" Jeff called, but he was too late.

Her mud-caked tennis shoes stepped into a murky puddle. "¡Ay!" she cried.

"Here, let me get those," he said, taking her flats.

"*Gracias*," she said softly.

"*De nada.*" Setting her flats on Alexa's scale, he wondered how Carmen would dry her soaking shoes. Did she even have another pair?

As the pickers completed their rows, they lined up at the scales with an odd assortment of partially filled flats. Jeff looked at their tired faces. Some nodded to him.

He tied down the truck and was double-checking his knots when he heard someone walk up behind him.

"Um, if you're not busy tomorrow," Alexa said, "we're going to have a barbecue at our picnic grounds." Jeff turned and she pointed across the lake to a large green lawn. He could see tables beneath an open-sided structure. There was a tiny building, a stone fire ring, and a volleyball net set up.

"It's for our full-time crew. Sort of a thank-you for the long days ahead."

If he accepted, Jeff thought, what exactly did that mean? Shouldn't he spend Sunday with Debbie? Yeah, but . . . He took a deep breath and checked a knot for the third time. "What about the weather?"

Alexa studied the sky. Jeff followed her eyes. Large patches of blue sky mixed with puffy clouds.

His mind jumped around searching for the right answer. Gut reaction, McKenzie. Go gut. He stuffed the loose rope beneath a pallet, then looked at Alexa.

She smiled cautiously.

"Sure."

Chapter 15

JEFF'S DAD FOLDED THE Sunday sports section and flopped it on the kitchen table. "I can't believe you missed the Eugene tournament yesterday."

Jeff dropped into a chair. "I had to work."

"Jason lost his doubles match." It was a matter-of-fact statement, but Jeff caught the hint of blame.

"Aaron Halvorson cleaned up," his dad continued. "Looks like he'll be strong at the Fourth of July Invitational."

Pile on the guilt, Jeff thought. Maybe it'll improve my game. He grabbed the paper and scanned the results. His stomach churned and he closed his eyes.

"Jeffery," he heard his mother, "Mrs. Halvorson said the coach from University of Oregon was there."

"Not a good one to miss." His dad tried to sound nonchalant. "You're practicing today, aren't you?"

Jeff opened his eyes.

"Aren't you?"

He sighed. "Yeah, I'm practicing."

"What about Debbie?" His mother set plates on the table.

"I don't know," he mumbled.

"You don't know?" She paused, holding a syrup bottle in midair like she was advertising it. "Well, if you practice this morning, that'll leave this afternoon and evening to spend with her." She waited.

"I'm going out to the farm this afternoon."

"The farm?" His dad took off his glasses and began wiping them with a napkin. "A little overtime to pay off your debt?"

"Not exactly."

"What then?"

"I'm going to a barbecue."

Hid dad put his glasses back on. "Isn't that going a bit far?"

"What do you mean?"

"Spending free time out there."

Jeff's mother set the syrup on the table. "Don't you want to see Debbie?"

Jeff's jaw was so tight he wasn't sure he could speak.

His mother raised her eyebrows.

"Don't worry about Debbie," he said flatly. He opened the newspaper again, hoping to end the conversation.

"All I know is," said his mother, "you two almost broke up after Palm Springs. That was hard on everyone."

Mark wandered into the kitchen. "It wasn't hard on me."

"No one asked you," said Jeff.

"Will the Mexicans be at this barbecue?" His dad crossed his arms and leaned forward on the table.

"Barbecue?" Mark asked hopefully.

"Not you." Jeff glared.

"What about the Mexicans?" his dad repeated.

"Beaners at a barbecue," Mark sing-songed. "That makes sense."

"Shut up!" Jeff snapped. "So what about the Mexicans?" He eyed his father. "What difference does it make?"

"You'll have tortillas instead of buns—yuck." Mark scrunched up his face.

Jeff stood up, knocking his chair against the wall. "You guys make me sick. You know your problem? I'll tell you," he said, without pausing. "You're racist."

Mark held up his hands. "Just joking."

"Jeffery," said his father. "I've told you before, I am not racist. I just see the Mexicans' shortcomings and I call them as I see them."

"Then don't generalize, Dad. Mexicans are individuals." He jerked his chair to the table and shoved the screen door open.

Jeff drove slowly through the Hampton's barnyard. Thick blackberry vines heavy with white blossoms lined the dusty road skirting the lake. Occasional stray canes stretched out from the wires, scratching their thorny fingers on his car.

A sloping lawn expanded between the road and the water. Libby and a group of workers were playing volleyball. Someone hit the ball into the net and everyone whooped and laughed.

"Welcome," Mrs. Hampton said as he got out of his car. She was missing her clipboard and whistle.

"Howdy, Jeff." Mr. Hampton waved a turner from behind the brick barbecue. He'd traded a work shirt for a pale blue T-shirt with a whale on it, but he still wore jeans and his pager. "How do you like your hamburger?"

"Any way is fine, thanks."

Jeff had figured that shorts, a T-shirt, and tennis shoes would be all right for today. It felt weird, though, driving down Bethel Road without the weight of his boot on the gas pedal.

"Libby, yell at Alexa to come in. These will be ready in a few minutes." Mr. Hampton began flipping the hamburgers.

Libby ran across the grass and onto the dock. "Alexa! Allexaaaa!" she shouted to a figure swimming the length of the lake. "Dad," she hollered back, "she's got her dumb cap on. She'll never hear me."

"She'll come when she's hungry."

Mrs. Hampton motioned Jeff to an empty lawn chair. "Would you like something to drink?"

"Sure. Thanks."

A chorus of groans arose from the volleyball game. The ball was bobbing in the water, moving quickly away from shore. There was a round of laughter and finger pointing, then everyone called to Alexa.

She changed direction, moving into a racing freestyle. No blond hair streamed behind her this time. All Jeff could see was a white cap, jetting through the water, and he wondered if she ever came up for air.

Alexa intercepted the ball and tucked it under her arm as if rescuing a drowning victim. She headed for the picnic grounds, slipping into a sidestroke with her free arm. Cheers greeted her as she stepped gingerly up the rocky bank and tossed the dripping ball into the group.

Jeff stared. "What does she have on?"

"Quite an outfit, isn't it?" Mrs. Hampton said.

Besides the tight white cap, Alexa wore small, beady-eyed goggles. She had three or four suits on, with large knots poking straight out in all directions.

"That's her drag suit, or suits I guess I should say." Mrs. Hampton shook her head. "The kids use their old suits to practice in. The more layers, the more resistance in the water."

"She's on a team?" Jeff asked.

"At Sheridan High."

"Come and get it! *¡Hamburguesas!* Hot dogs! You want it we got it!" Mr. Hampton called.

The volleyballers strolled toward the barbecue. "*¿Cómo estás?*" Macario greeted Jeff.

"*Bien, gracias.*"

"This is Jeff McKenzie—*muy buen chófer*," he told the group.

"He says you are a very good truck driver." Mr. Hampton slapped hamburgers into buns and set them on paper plates. "Come on you guys. The introductions are going to have to wait. These are gonna get cold."

"Go on, Jeff, get yourself something to eat," said Mrs. Hampton. "All the fixings are here on the table and there's some salads and chips and a cake."

"And s'mores when Dad builds a fire," said Libby, squirting mustard on her hamburger.

Jeff was about to join the line when he saw Alexa walking up from the lake. She'd pulled off her cap and goggles and was wiping her arms with a large beach towel. Her tangled hair fell carelessly across her shoulders. "I didn't know you were here," she said, wrapping the towel around her waist.

"I didn't know you swam." Jeff tried to keep his eyes on her face but he could see droplets of water slipping down her chest and the shape of her breasts, pressed tight against her suits.

She looked at him, puzzled.

"I mean," he stumbled, "competitively. Your mom

says you're on the Sheridan team."

"Uh-huh." She combed her hands through her hair. "We'd better get something to eat. Dad gets pretty testy if we don't come when it's hot."

"So what do you swim?" Jeff asked as they moved toward the barbecue.

"Five-hundred-yard freestyle, two-hundred breaststroke, and the individual medley."

"Geez, you must be good."

Water dripped from her bangs onto her cheek. She wiped it off and shrugged.

"Well, are you?"

"I guess so."

"What does that mean?"

Alexa cleared her throat. "I took state in the five-hundred freestyle."

"So what the heck are you doing here? Shouldn't you be going to matches? Getting ready for the Olympics or something?"

"They're meets, not matches."

"Okay, whatever." He watched as she cut her hamburger. "I think you're wasting time."

"There are some club meets I can go to in the summer," she said, licking her finger, "but they get expensive. Besides, can you imagine my family taking off during harvest?"

"Do you want to go pro?" He glanced around for a place to sit.

"There is no professional swimming. The Olympics and World Championships are as high as you can get." Alexa moved toward a large, round wooden table. "Let's join these guys."

"Don't you resent it?" asked Jeff.

"What?" said Alexa.

"That you can't compete in the summer."

"Not really. I get plenty of swimming in during the school year."

Santiago was in the midst of a story in rapid-fire Spanish.

Squeezing in between Alexa and Macario, Jeff felt her damp towel against his leg. "Do you know what he's saying?" Jeff whispered.

"No. When they get going that fast I'm lost." Her face was so close he could see tiny freckles on her nose.

Now Santiago was using his hands in time with his voice. He lifted his eyebrows and tilted his head. This was how Macario often spoke when he had a lot to say, as if his entire body was sending the message.

Santiago took a sip of pop and appeared to be through.

"Macario, what's so funny?" Alexa asked.

"He tells about his nickname '*licenciado*.'" Macario reached for a bowl of salsa. "When he is small boy, our family is very poor. Someone gives him suit—you know, the kind *importante* person wears. He likes the suit very much but no *especial* place to wear it, so he wear it any-way, maybe just to play in. Somebody say he looks like little lawyer, so he is '*licenciado*.'"

Macario spooned salsa over his chips, then glanced around the table. "I tell you these people," he said to Jeff. He pointed at Santiago and Jerónimo, reminding Jeff they were his *hermanos*. "You meet *Chilango* yester-day," he said, nodding at Casimiro.

"¿*Chilango*?" Jeff looked at Casimiro who smiled now at the attention. His face seemed broader and smoother and shinier than those of the other Mexicans at the table. His long black hair was tied into place at the base of his neck with a leather shoelace, and he wore a University of Massachusetts T-shirt.

"*Chilango* is person from Mexico City," explained Macario, turning to the next man. "This is Hilario Espinoza, *mi tío*—my uncle, and Jesús Bautista, *mi cuñado*—my brother-in-law." Each smiled and nodded.

"*Gordito*," Santiago corrected, shaking a chip at Jesús. Everyone laughed.

Jesús grinned.

"*Sí*, little fat one," Macario translated.

"Geez, you guys," said Jeff. "We'd never get away with that at school. It'd be a referral for sure."

"This is *diferente*," said Macario. "We say just to our friends. You know, how you say things to persons just for fun, not for hurt."

"What's your nickname, Macario?" Jeff asked.

"No nickname."

"Oh, *sí*," protested Hilario. His graying hair stuck out from beneath a John Deere hat. He spoke to the others in Spanish and they all motioned agreement. "Macario, he is *abuelita*."

"Oh, yeah?" said Jeff.

Macario studied his plate.

Alexa choked, then laughed. "It means little grandmother."

"Little grandmother?" Jeff looked at Macario. "Give us the story."

Macario shook his head.

"Come on, let's hear it."

He answered slowly, "I am, what you say? Very careful? I am always the person to remind 'clean up the food, pick up the clothes, turn off the light.' At the *casa*," he nodded beyond the barnyard, "I tell these peoples many times to do these things. They are like little children."

The men watched closely, trying to follow Macario's English. He shrugged his shoulders. "I cannot be different."

"Sure you can," said Jeff. "Just lighten up, Macario."

"Lighten up?"

"Yeah—don't worry about it so much. Back off."

"*Calma*," said Hilario.

"*Paciencia*," added Jerónimo, pushing his plate away.

Alexa reached behind Jeff and patted Macario's back. "It's okay, Macario. Just say what my dad says when things aren't working."

"*¿Sí?*"

"He says, 'Oh, well.'"

"I'll bet he says more than that," said Jeff.

"Oh, well." Macario tried the words. "That, we say, is *ni modo*."

When they finished eating, some lingered around the table while others moved to the lawn, stretching out, groaning that they'd eaten too much. Macario introduced Jeff to Raúl, someone's nephew, and Venancio, the truck driver who'd sprained his ankle.

"How is your foot?" Jeff asked

Venancio quickly stood and walked proudly in a circle. "*Bien.*"

"Let's play soccer," announced Libby.

Macario held his stomach. "*Mucho comida.*"

"Please, Macario." She grabbed his hand.

"Okay, we play soccer," he said, coaxing the others.

The volleyball net and empty fire pit became goals. Jeff tried to hang back, but Macario motioned him into the group. "Is good for your tennis."

"You, too, Alexa," Jeff called as she stepped from the bath house, dressed in shorts and a tank top.

The game started, and Jeff was swept up in the running, bumping, kicking. He tried to watch the ball, but if he watched too long, he crashed into someone.

Once, the ball was right at his feet and, without

thinking, he gave it a swift kick, sending it above the opposition. Santiago stopped the fly ball with his head, laughing as he rubbed his scalp.

"¡*Que bueno!*" shouted Macario.

Jeff slipped into the game's rhythm: jog down the 'field,' jostle for position, control the ball. His body began to anticipate and react. He hit another shot: it smashed into the volleyball net. "All right!" He couldn't believe it felt good to hit a ball into a net.

The ball was in play again and bodies raced and dodged, hopped and turned. Jeff jumped aside, smacking into Alexa. She lost her balance and Jeff tripped over her. Both fell to the ground. He quickly rolled over. "Are you okay?" he asked, out of breath.

"Uh-huh."

Jeff helped her to her feet. She rubbed her knee and winced.

"Are you sure you're okay?"

"I'm fine."

The game resumed and a few minutes later the soccer ball soared into the lake.

"I'm dressed, you guys!" shouted Alexa before they could bargain with her.

Venancio ran for the canoe with both teams yelling directions.

Alexa stepped onto the wooden diving board.

Now what? Jeff wondered. Maybe it was time to leave. But it was nice to be with Alexa when they didn't have berries to weigh and load. He joined her on the diving board. "It's weird. I feel like I should be working."

"I know. It's hard to relax here. Dad always has an eye on the fields and the irrigation. He has to be at least two hours away for a real break."

"He could go to your swim meets," Jeff suggested.

"Alexa, you're an awesome swimmer. You've got to compete year-round."

"Maybe next year, when I have my license, I'll drive to a few meets."

"You're not getting your license now?"

"Are you kidding? Nothing happens during strawberry harvest. You saw my birthday party."

A fish broke the water's still surface and quickly retreated, sending out a rhythm of thin rings.

"Hey, guys, wanna go swimming?" Libby jumped onto the diving board.

"Not now, Lib," said Alexa.

Jeff suddenly wanted to be alone with Alexa. Anywhere. Just someplace where they could talk—or not talk—without interruption. He cleared his throat. "Alexa, let's practice for your test. We can take my Bronco."

"Me, too. I wanna go," Libby said.

"You don't need any practice," said Jeff. "I've seen you on the four-wheeler."

"But—"

"Maybe next time, okay, kid?" Jeff ruffled her hair.

Chapter 16

ALEXA SNAPPED HER SEAT BELT IN PLACE. "Ready?"
"Ready."

She maneuvered smoothly past the blackberries and through the barnyard. Swinging onto the road, she shifted into high gear.

"Hey, slow down, or you I'll make you wash my car," Jeff protested. "I should have known. You probably drove tractors before you could walk."

"Almost."

"Signal to turn," he directed, as Alexa pulled up to the stop sign across from the grain tanks.

"Signal? There's no one around for miles."

"That'll cost you points." Jeff licked his finger and marked the air.

Alexa rolled her eyes. She flipped on the signal and turned.

They drove for awhile without speaking. For as far as Jeff could see, fields cut into squares and rectangles with ditches and fence rows marking precise boundaries. "You know," he mused, "everything seems so perfect out here."

"What do you mean?"

"I'm not sure. It's just a feeling. Everything seems to have a place. It's peaceful."

"If you want peaceful—there it is." She pointed out her window.

"The oak grove?"

"Uh-huh."

"What about it?"

"Lib and I used to ride our horses here." She paused a moment as if debating with herself. Then she continued with a faint smile. "We'd pack our lunch boxes and fill Dad's old Boy Scout canteens and pretend we were going to Alaska. We'd make wilderness forts and live off the land."

"I never did anything like that."

"That's not true." Alexa pulled off the road and stopped. "All kids play fort and castle and house."

"Not if you're going to tennis lessons and piano lessons and golf lessons."

"Not all the time."

"That's what I remember." He took a deep breath and reached for the door handle. "Let's check out Alaska."

Jeff held the barbed wire fence down for Alexa and followed her through tall grass into the cool, dark circle of oaks. A shaft of sunlight pierced through a break in the leafy ceiling, sending a sparkling ray straight to the ground. "We called that fairy dust." Her eyes wandered among the trees as if taking inventory. "Our cabin was over there. See that low branch? It curves up? Libby called it her special seat. She'd sit there and order me around. 'Today,'" Alexa mimicked her sister, "'you need to cut wood for the winter and catch something to eat.'"

Alexa climbed onto the curved limb, and Jeff sat on the ground beside her, leaning against the tree trunk. He picked up a twig and began stirring in the dirt.

"Fixing dinner?" Alexa asked.

"Yeah—spaghetti."

"You're getting the hang of this. Maybe you're not as deprived up as I thought." She stopped, then whispered, "Look."

He turned his head cautiously. There, standing between two trees, was a doe and a fawn. Straight-legged, they stared from their post, ears alert. Then the mother casually bent her head, tore off a tuft of grass, raised her head back up and began chewing and flicking her ears. The fawn sniffed the ground and chose a dry leaf.

A few minutes later, the deer ambled away through the trees.

Jeff turned back, his eyes meeting Alexa's. "That was awesome," he whispered.

Alexa nodded slowly, her eyes remaining on his for an extra moment.

★   ★   ★

Macario was leaving the barnyard as Jeff and Alexa pulled in.

"Is everyone gone?" Alexa asked, stopping next to his pickup.

"No. Mr. Hampton, he is making a fire for Libby. I have to move sprinklers in the corn. Mr. Hampton, he says to show Jeff the pipe moving."

"I didn't bring any work clothes," said Jeff.

"No problem," said Alexa. "You can wear Dad's rubber boots." She gave him a sidelong glance. "I'll help. This could be pretty funny."

"That's the thanks I get for a driving lesson?"

"What lesson?" Alexa ran into the house. When she reappeared, she held up a pair of boots in each hand.

Tossing them into the back of Macario's pickup, she motioned Jeff to the cab. Except for one Spanish cassette tape on the dash, the inside was spotless and smelled of pine tree air freshener.

Macario entered the cornfield on the east side of Bethel Road and drove halfway up the edge. Once stopped, Jeff and Alexa sat on the bumper, pulled off their tennis shoes, and slipped on the rubber boots.

"You have a farmer's tan," Alexa said, examining his legs and arms.

He rolled up his T-shirt sleeve.

"Uh-huh. Farmer's tan."

"Well, let's see," said Jeff, leaning back against the tailgate. "I've unplugged the urinal, I've lost flats on the highway, I've picked strawberries, and now I have a farmer's tan—all in about two weeks. Does that make up for the bean field?"

Alexa stood up. "Let's see how you move irrigation pipe."

They followed Macario along a large pipe that stretched across the field. Every sixty feet or so they passed a valve sticking up from the pipe. When they reached the first row of sprinklers, Macario twisted a T-handle on the connecting valve. Water spraying from the sprinklers slowed to a weak drizzle, then to just a drip. As Macario flipped up a latch on the valve, Alexa hurried down to the first riser and disconnected another latch.

"*Gracias,*" Macario called, moving to the middle of the smaller pipe. He picked it up, balanced it like a tightrope walker, and headed for the next valve.

"I'll unhook another pipe," Alexa told Jeff. A few seconds later, she called, "Okay, pick up your end."

The pipe was lighter than Jeff expected. They

tromped across the field, stepping over ankle-high corn-stalks. Jeff shoved the pipe into Macario's and flipped the latch down over a small metal tip.

Alexa tugged her end before setting it down. "It's got to be really tight, otherwise it'll leak or break loose."

As they returned for the next pipe, Alexa called, "Show Jeff one-handed."

Macario shifted the pipe, dropped a hand to his side, and began jogging.

"I gotta try that," said Jeff, centering himself behind the pipe.

She raised her eyebrows. "Are you sure?" She unhooked the latch.

"Sure." Jeff stretched out his arms and slipped his hands under the three-inch aluminum tube. With a firm grip, he lifted. The pipe immediately rolled forward, the weight of the riser swinging the sprinkler head down, crashing into the ground.

Alexa burst out laughing. She tried to walk, but stopped to cross her rubber boots. "I'm going to wet my pants."

"I'm glad I'm so entertaining," Jeff said dryly. He moved his hands down the pipe, searching for the balance point. Then, cupping the pipe in a tight hold, he marched across the field.

Once the entire line had been moved, Jeff and Alexa joined Macario at the valve.

"You do it," Macario told Jeff. "Twist to open." Jeff bent and grasped the cold steel handle. He gave it a sharp, counterclockwise jerk. Hissing rushed from the seals. Jeff stopped.

"The water, it is pushing the air," said Macario. "Keep going."

Water dribbled from the base of the valve and the

hissing noise continued down the sprinkler line as Jeff turned it five or six more times. Sprinkler heads began moving, water trickled out, then arched, and finally, with a sudden spurt, kicked into full spray. The air filled with the strong *tsh tsh tsh* of sprinkler heads whacking against propelling water. Sunlight flashed off the droplets and rainbow colors glistened in the mist above the water line.

"I like the water," said Macario. "It is very beautiful to me."

Jeff watched as the row of sprinklers turned in separate, unsynchronized circles. "Do they ever line up," he asked, "so they all go around at the same time?"

"No," said Macario, "but they all work together to do the same job."

For a moment they watched the sprinklers, ticking and spraying. Jeff felt himself hypnotized with the pulsating movement.

"When I was born," Alexa said, her eyes still steady on the water, "some farmer told Dad it was too bad he didn't get his pipe mover."

"You mean a boy?"

"Yeah." Alexa's head moved slowly as she inspected the farm. "Dad said, 'You bet I did.'" She looked at Jeff. "Someday I'm going to run this place—that'll show 'em."

"You?"

She frowned. "Yeah, *me*."

"Sorry, I just haven't met many girl farmers."

"Well, now you've met one." She held out her hand.

Jeff looked in her determined eyes. Her face was flushed and wisps of hair flicked across her cheek. He reached for her hand and grasped it. He felt the callous on the inside of her right palm and a knot at the back of his throat.

A speckled hawk cried out above them, closely followed by two harassing swallows. Alexa squeezed Jeff's hand, then let go.

"Poor bird," she said. "Why are they after him?"

"Maybe they are afraid he will take their food," said Macario.

The hawk dipped down, banked right, and then swung up, but the swallows stayed with him.

"I am like the big bird, sometimes," Macario said so softly Jeff barely heard him.

"What do you mean?" Jeff asked uneasily.

"You know, how people can be mean in the little ways. Always saying things, or writing things, like a little pin, hitting at your skin." He pretended to poke at his arm.

"Can't you fight back?"

"Most of the times, you just live with it, pretend it is not there. You make a wall in your mind and you don't listen."

"But don't you ever stand up for yourself?"

"You must decide, must think," said Macario, tapping his head, "what is most important at the time. Is it worth a fight? Can you protect yourself?"

Jeff's eyes wandered across the cornfield, past the boysenberries, and settled on the spray-painted grain tanks. "What about the 'wetback' stuff? Doesn't that make you mad?"

"'Wetback' is no *problema*. With immigration laws, I am okay to be here. I am legal person in United States. I can walk across the line instead of running at night. I can smile to the border patrol and say, "*Buenos días*."

Macario put his hands in his back pockets and breathed in the evening air. "Sometimes I fly from Guadalajara in the big airplane to Portland. I get the peanuts and Pepsi and two lunches.

"*Problema*," he said, turning serious, "is how you say 'wetback.'" Like the nicknames. If you my friend and only tease then maybe is okay. If you try to hurt me, then is not okay."

Jeff glanced once more at the sky. Was the hawk ignoring the persistent swallows? Would it ever fight back? Or would the swallows tire of the routine and fly away, leaving the hawk to search peaceably for its food and to soar free?

Chapter 17

MARTHA'S PARKING LOT WAS CROWDED. A couple more vans than normal, a few more cars. Two black Labs sat patiently in the rear of a small pickup.

Inside the store customers stood around the coffeepot or browsed through the newspaper rack. Some sat at white plastic tables smoking cigarettes and eating doughnuts.

"You're up bright and early, cutie," said Martha. "Got a hot date?"

Jeff checked the myrtlewood clock behind the counter. He'd stopped wearing a watch awhile back—it only got wet, scratched or slimed. He'd learned that once he arrived at the field, the rest of the day hung on the berries, not on the hands of a clock.

"*Hola,*" said a man standing at the counter.

"*Hola.*" Jeff recognized many of the men now. They worked at a nursery another mile or two out of town, and they stopped daily at Martha's for orange juice, coffee, and powdered-sugar doughnuts.

"*¿Cómo está?*" someone asked.

"*Bien.*"

"Ah, *mucho español.*"

"*No mucho.*" Jeff shook his head.

The guys at the nearest table laughed.

Jeff poured coffee into a large Styrofoam cup, clamped on a lid, and set fifty cents on the counter.

"This rain affect your berries?" asked Martha.

"There's more rot in the field, and we're down pickers."

"You'll have more today," she said. "The rain cracked most of the cherry crop, and some farmers have quit harvesting."

Mr. Hampton's pickup, Macario's pickup, and a four-wheeler were parked along the edge of the cornfield where, less than twelve hours ago, Jeff had moved pipe.

Mr. Hampton stood at the same valve Jeff had turned on last night. Macario and Jerónimo were inspecting the sprinkler line. Jeff swallowed hard. Whatever's wrong, he thought, please don't let it be my fault. He turned onto the headland and drove slowly up the north side.

"Oh, no," he groaned as he spotted the washout, spreading from the valve, past the sprinklers, down the rows, carving deep, muddy ravines. Walking out to the damage, he winced at the baby cornstalks smashed in the mud and sprinklers turned on their sides.

"What happened?"

"Vandals," said Mr. Hampton. "Someone kicked the sprinkler off the valve opener. Looks like water poured out for at least half the night."

Jeff released a slow breath. He almost felt guilty for being so relieved.

★　★　★

133

"Do you always have this much vandalism?" Jeff asked Alexa as she slipped the green yarn and silver punch around her neck.

"Including yours?"

Jeff grimaced. "Give me a break. I didn't aim for the pump. Any idea who did it?"

"No."

"How about that Mexican you fired?"

"I doubt it."

"Why?"

Alexa shrugged.

"He stole from you at least two times."

"Yes, but he wouldn't have painted the grain tanks."

"So, maybe there's more than one person doing all this."

Libby pounded her scale like a drum. "I bet I know."

"Who?" Jeff and Alexa asked in unison.

"Corey."

"Forget it." Alexa glared at her sister.

"Who's Corey?" asked Jeff.

"He's—" Libby started.

"Nobody," Alexa finished.

No one had time that day to solve the latest attack. More people showed up, even though it was the third pick. Mrs. Hampton confirmed Martha's news about the cherry disaster.

"But how could one lousy day of rain do all that damage?" Jeff asked.

"Timing," she said. "A week ago, it wouldn't have mattered. But the cherries were nice and ripe. And don't forget about the humidity Saturday—it's as dangerous at the rain."

New pickers. Third pick. Bad combination.

At lunch, Ethel slumped into her chair. "Cherry pickers are not berry pickers."

"They specialize?" Jeff asked.

"Not exactly." Ethel breathed on her sunglasses and rubbed them with her T-shirt. "Some just have a crop they prefer."

"True," said Mrs. Hampton, "but their background also makes a difference. Those from the mountain areas of Jalisco, especially around Atotonilco, are familiar with orchard work—lots of lime trees. They handle ladders well, moving them, setting them up, picking from them. The people from the Guanajuato area, however, are used to field crops, like strawberries."

"I was a darn recording all morning," said Ethel, "telling everyone the fruit was as good—or as crummy— on any given row and they couldn't go roaming around looking for *the* best spot."

"Tell them we're paying two cents more a pound," said Mrs. Hampton.

Alexa leaned against her scale, studying the field entrance. "Guess we've got another u-picker who can't read. She glanced at Jeff. "Ready to direct traffic?"

"Ready." He looked to the main road, then froze. Oh, God, he thought, not here, not now.

★   ★   ★

The red CRX came to a stop at the crossroads.

Debbie.

Jeff stared at her white shorts and pink tank top. Was this going to be friendly? With picking Saturday and the barbecue Sunday, he hadn't seen Debbie at all that weekend. He'd even forgotten to call. He sucked in a deep breath, realizing suddenly that Alexa had no clue. Way to go, McKenzie.

Now he cringed as Debbie tiptoed in her white sandals through the rutted road. She held a wicker basket in one hand. "Hi! I brought you lunch."

Jeff walked up to her. "Howdy."

"Howdy?" she laughed. "Don't I get more than a 'howdy?'" She reached up and kissed him behind the ear.

"You're going to get dirty if you get any closer."

She looked him over. "You *are* a mess, aren't you?"

"Who's that?" Libby whispered loudly.

"Beats me," Ethel answered.

"Didn't you see the sign?" Jeff pointed to the entrance.

"Honestly, I wasn't about to walk all the way in here. Now, don't just stand there—introduce me." She slipped her arm around his elbow.

Jeff swallowed and turned back to the group. The spark had left Libby's face and her mouth hung open. Ethel began rummaging around in her cooler.

"Hi, I'm Maggie Hampton. Your timing couldn't be better."

You've got to be joking, Jeff thought. "This is my, uh, friend Debbie Norton," he said.

Libby shut her mouth. Ethel nodded.

Jeff started to introduce Alexa, but she cut in. "I'm Alexa Hampton," she said firmly, her eyes avoiding Jeff's.

"Hi." Debbie studied Alexa, then placed her arm around Jeff's waist, smiling. "I just had to make sure he was getting a decent meal and not working himself into the ground." Turning to Jeff, she said, "Why don't we find some secluded spot for our picnic?"

"Maybe I'll show Debbie the dam," he said to no one in particular. He shifted uneasily from one foot to the other. "I'll be back in a bit."

"That's fine, Jeff," said Mrs. Hampton. "Take longer if you want."

"High maintenance," he heard Ethel mutter as he led Debbie to her car.

He kicked the mud off his boots and climbed in the passenger side. "Go straight and turn right on the headland."

"'Headland'—oooh, such big farm talk—I don't know what a headland is." Debbie flipped on the radio.

Jeff's shoulders tensed. "It's the open space at the end of the rows where the tractor turns around."

"You've really picked up this stuff, huh? How's it going?"

"Fine." He directed her along the cattails toward the end of the lake. The cattails thinned out and the steep bank dropped to a wooden platform where two gray pumps hummed and water surged through huge pipes. The lake was perfectly still, reflecting sky and clouds. "Pretty, isn't it?" Jeff mused aloud.

"Looks cold." Debbie parked her car.

"It's not bad." He led the way through tall grass and weeds.

"Ow, ooh."

"Why did you wear sandals?"

"Well, it's a warm day, isn't it?"

"Right." Jeff stomped the grass flat beneath one of the trees.

"You know, Jeff, you sure don't seem very happy to see me. We did this all the time last summer. Remember?"

"I'm busier this summer," he said curtly, then regretted it. She'd packed a lunch and come all this way, and he was acting like a jerk. "I'm sorry. There's just so much going on, lots of problems . . . "

"Here. I even brought a little tablecloth." She spread the red-and-white checkered material over the trampled grass.

"Not exactly the country club, but it'll do." She took out plastic baggies and containers. "There's ham sandwiches and potato salad and white chocolate chip cookies, and . . . " she paused, ". . . a little thirst quencher." She pulled out two beers.

Jeff felt strange sitting down beside her. But why? This should be the best thing to happen in days. Debbie, lunch, a cold beer. Almost like old times. Except he was in jeans instead of tennis shorts and the view was of a lake instead of a swimming pool.

He took the beer can and snapped the tab. Foam spilled out.

"To your next match." Debbie toasted, tapping her can against his.

Jeff slowly took a sip. Then he stood up. He gazed across the lake to the floating raft and to the Hampton's picnic ground. The canoe lay overturned on the grass. A fish wind sock fluttered from the bath house. His eyes drifted to the volleyball net. Or was it a soccer net? He looked up to the timbered foothills and then to the Coast Range, almost silver now in the afternoon sun.

"Earth to Jeff."

"Oh, sorry, Deb. Uh—do you have a Coke or something? I think I'll pass on the beer."

"You're kidding, right? It's nice and cold." She rolled her eyes. "If I'd known, I could have picked up a pop at that little hick grocery store when I asked for directions."

"Martha's Market?"

"Something like that. The woman in charge is some wacko with a weird eye. Gave me the once over when I asked how to get here."

"Martha's pretty sharp." Jeff almost laughed at the thought of Martha directing Debbie.

"Those Mexicans hanging around her place, they really checked me out. What a bunch of creeps."

"Geez, Debbie, give them a break. Who wouldn't look? You barely have anything on."

"You're defending a bunch of Mexicans you don't even know? Give *me* a break, McKenzie."

Jeff stared.

"Listen. I came out here to talk. I don't think we've been on the same wavelength." She patted the tablecloth. "Sit down."

Jeff settled cross-legged and accepted a sandwich.

"Cindy's having another party Friday night," Debbie said. "Why don't we go and spend time together?"

"Sure."

"I went to your match in Eugene, Saturday, but you weren't there."

"You drove all the way to Eugene?"

"Uh-huh." She took a bite of her sandwich.

"I had no idea you'd be going."

"See, Jeff, we don't even talk." Debbie set her sandwich down. "In case you haven't noticed, you haven't been a whole lot of fun lately."

"Deb, listen, I'm sorry, okay? But there's not much I can do about it. Just hang in there; it'll be over soon."

"But I'm used to seeing you every day. This has really gotten old fast. I don't like going to things without you."

Jeff shivered. He hated whining.

"There's a rumor we've broken up."

"Don't listen, Debbie."

"Well, it's embarrassing, and it doesn't feel so great when a bunch of crummy strawberries get more attention than I do." She bristled. "Or . . . or maybe it's that farmer's daughter."

"What?" He threw his sandwich down.

"A little young for you, isn't she?"

"She's sixteen. She just looks younger without gobs of makeup on."

Debbie ignored the comment. "Looks to me like this is a favorite spot down here."

Jeff stood and followed her glare to a neat pile of blankets and two pillows set next to the base of a tree.

"Those are not mine," he said tersely.

"Whose are they?"

"I—I don't know," he stumbled. "I mean, I can't say."

"What?"

"I was asked not to say anything."

"You can't tell me about a few lousy blankets? This is getting pretty ridiculous."

Jeff picked up his beer and poured it into a foaming puddle. "I'm not sure about Cindy's party," he said steadily. "I never know when I'll get back from the cannery, and I might have to move irrigation pipe. Besides, I've got a tennis match Saturday."

"I know—Aaron told me." Debbie tossed plastic forks and paper plates into the basket. "So this is the thanks I get for coming out here, trying to jazz up our relationship. I even washed my car this morning. Now it's filthy."

"You're welcome to stay, Debbie. We could use another picker, and then you could ride to the cannery with me."

"Funny, real funny."

He picked up the tablecloth, but Debbie snatched it from his hands. "I don't know what's come over you, McKenzie. I think the country air is getting to you." Grabbing the picnic basket, she stomped through the grass. "Ouch! Damn!" She hopped on one foot and rubbed the other.

They drove in silence to the field. "Sorry if I ruined your picnic," Jeff said, shutting the car door. "Thanks for coming."

Debbie stared straight ahead.

"Listen, maybe we can still work this out."

"Something *is* going to work out." Debbie crammed the gearshift into first. "Aaron said that if you don't have time for me, he does. I just might take him up on it."

"So Aaron's in on this, huh? I should have known." He scuffed his boot in the dirt. "Okay, maybe Aaron can do a better job."

"Don't say I didn't try." Her eyes narrowed. "And don't think your mom can put this one back together."

"What are you talking about?"

"I'm talking about Palm Springs. We almost broke up, remember? In case you didn't know, your mother called, explaining how much you missed me and needed me in your life. She said you were sending flowers."

"Flowers?"

"Yeah, but I never got any."

Jeff stepped back from the car.

Chapter 18

JEFF STOOD MOTIONLESS in the middle of the dirt road. What do I say now? My girlfriend brought me lunch and a beer but I didn't drink the beer and we broke up. Because you wouldn't drink the beer? No, not exactly.

The sound of a Spanish radio station drifted over the rows. Jeff breathed in the warm afternoon air and turned for the truck.

"Was that your girlfriend?" Libby dangled her legs from the end of the flatbed.

Alexa's questioning eyes rested on his for a moment, then looked away.

"Yeah," Jeff said. "Was."

"Whatdaya mean?"

"Well, let's just say we didn't have the world's greatest picnic."

"Did you get in a fight?"

"Uhh—"

"Libby, that's prying," Mrs. Hampton warned.

"It's okay," said Jeff. "Yeah, I guess we did."

"You guess?" said Libby. "You were there, right?"

Jeff laughed. "Okay. Okay. We had a fight."

"Did you break up?"

"Geez Lib, give the guy some space," Alexa said.

"Relax," Libby defended, "I'm just asking."

Alexa tossed a paper sack in the nearby garbage can. "When's your next tournament?"

"Saturday. Corvallis Swim and Tennis Club. It could be pretty ugly," he said, shaking his head. "By then, it will have been two weeks since I've competed." He grimaced. "And, it'll be my last competition before the Fourth of July Invitational." He looked hopefully at Mrs. Hampton.

"I don't see a problem," she said.

"What's so big about the Invitational?" Libby mumbled.

"Tradition." Jeff made a seat of empty flats. "Been going on for a zillion years. Lots of fancy trophies. The club goes all out—decorations, barbecue, live band."

"Sounds cool."

"It's pretty cool." Jeff held back a smile. "The major thing for me is beating this guy Sam Nelson."

"Why?" asked Alexa.

"He's from Portland. Plays for a classy club. Thinks he's pretty hot stuff. I've played him so many times I've lost count. We go back and forth winning and losing. He took the Invitational trophy last year, so I'm under a lot of pressure to get it back—if I make it to the finals."

"Can we come?" asked Libby.

"Just invite yourself," said Alexa.

"Yeah, you can come," said Jeff.

Libby sat up straight and brushed her hair back. "Are we supposed to wear white clothes?"

Jeff shrugged. "I don't pay much attention, but it seems people dress up."

"Mom, can I get a new white outfit?"

"I think you probably have something to wear."

"Aww, Mom, come on."

"We'll see."

"That means 'no.'" Libby scowled.

"Oh—the Fourth—I forgot," said Mrs. Hampton. "We've got tickets to the St. Paul Rodeo."

"What time?" asked Jeff.

"7:30."

"The tournament goes all day but it should be over by five or six." Jeff rolled up his T-shirt sleeves. "It would be great if you could all come."

Mrs. Hampton smiled. "Thank you for the invitation, Jeff. Let's see what happens. We've still got two weeks."

★ ★ ★

Macario drove the GMC into the field.

"Good timing," Jeff said, jerking on his last knot. "You must have ESP."

"ESP?"

"Yeah—extrasensory perception. It's when you know when something's going to happen. We were going to need the GMC in a few minutes."

"Maybe I have the E-S-P and the G-M-C, but I also have the radio." He patted his handheld strapped to his side. "Mrs. Hampton, she talked to me."

"Oh, right. I forgot."

Macario quickly examined the truck. "It's good."

Jeff felt a sudden surge of pride. "Thanks." He leaned against the rear of the truck.

"Uh, Macario, is there, maybe, any chance you could come to my tennis tournament on the Fourth of July?" As soon as the words were out he wondered what he was doing, asking everyone to the Invitational. How could he play a decent game with Macario and Alexa watching?

"I would like to go very much. But, I do not know for sure. Maybe too much work."

"Geez, you sound like Cinderella."

"Ah, *la Cenicienta*. No," he said, shaking his head, "you have the wrong story. Mr. and Mrs. Hampton, they are not mean like the *feas* stepsisters."

"I know Mrs. Hampton's nice, but Mr. Hampton still makes me nervous."

Macario leaned against the truck, next to Jeff. "You don't know what a good person is *Don* Jake."

"*¿Don?*"

"*Sí*. It is highest respect. More higher than *señor*. I tell you, when I first come to Oregon, maybe sixteen years ago, I hear of job in Mt. Hood National Forest, planting trees." He fussed with the end of a rope. "I have no money, no food. The labor contractor, he gives us plastic to make tents. He gives us bag of corn flour and a gun. He tell us to shoot a deer. We did. But there is no refrigerator. So, every day, we just smell the deer to see if it is getting bad."

"That's disgusting."

"*Sí*. I don't like killing the deers and skinning—especially if the mothers, when you open, you find a baby."

Jeff's stomach lurched.

"But the other *problema* is, the contractor he say the forest service is not happy with our job and there is no pay. The workers, we say we will do it over again. We did. Still, the contractor, he say it is not done the right way and no money. We leave, without a penny. We find out later, the contractor is paid, but he keeps our money."

"What'd you do?"

"I hear of Mr. Hampton. He has good name for taking

care of his workers. He give me a job, place to stay, pay me every two weeks. I send money to *mi familia*. I go back to Mexico in *octubre* with dresses for *mi esposa*, jackets for the *niños*, shoes, thread, fabric, a radio, and I help to buy the first tractor for the *rancho*." Macario smiled. "If Mr. Hampton say he needs me to work Fourth of July, I will work."

Jeff nodded.

"So now, you go to cannery. *Que te vaya bien*."

"Thanks."

Macario turned back. "Mr. Hampton, he usually gives us the holidays for not working."

Chapter 19

AT LUNCH THE NEXT DAY Macario roared into the berry field on a four-wheeler. "You come with me?" he asked Jeff.

"Yeah, I guess so." Jeff hopped off the truck and looked in question at Alexa.

She shrugged her shoulders.

"We take the *mosca*."

"The what?"

"*Mosca*." Macario pointed to the four-wheeler. "Is Spanish for 'fly,' you know, the *insecto*."

Jeff climbed on behind Macario. They drove toward the lake and along the headland past the cornfield. Someone was cultivating between the corn rows with a small red tractor.

"*Avispa*," said Macario. "The tractor, see, it looks like a wasp." Jeff squinted, trying to imagine a broad head and long body.

Macario zipped by the boysenberries, around the tip of the lake, and into the barnyard.

Jesús, Hilario, and Venancio stood outside the large

machinery shed, washing their hands under a faucet. Jesús waved a dripping hand.

Jeff smelled the heavy aroma of meat and onions frying. His stomach urged him to walk toward the shop, but instead, Macario led the way to the far end of the machinery shed. There, with one end tied around a metal fence post, and the other around a maple tree, was the volleyball net, stretched low to the ground. Farm machinery had been moved to the edge of the blackberry field and clumps of weeds were piled in a corner.

"Is tennis court," announced Macario proudly.

The others joined them. Santiago held two rackets in his hand and Jerónimo carried a can of balls.

"Where'd you get these?" Jeff asked. The rackets had seen better days: the wooden frames were scraped and nicked and the strings were loose.

"We find them at Goodwill—in Sheridan." Santiago struggled for the right words, then grinned.

"They're great, just great," said Jeff.

"You can practice more now on the farm," said Macario.

Jeff took one of the rackets and opened the can of balls. They, too, were well-used, but still had a little life. He walked onto the dirt court and studied the volleyball net. A bit high. He tossed a ball in the air, swung the racket back, up over his head, and slammed through the ball. It flew across the net, bounced once, and hit the metal building. Casimiro retrieved the ball.

"Did it hurt the building?" called Jeff.

Macario interpreted and Casimiro inspected. No, he shook his head.

Jeff handed the other racket to Macario. "Now I can show you something. Hold it with your thumb and fore-finger making a V along this edge." He placed Macario's hand in the correct position, then stepped back. "Now bend your knees and hold the racket in front of you like this—it's called the 'ready position.'"

The others laughed as Macario awkwardly bent his knees and stiffly held his racket away from his body.

Jeff explained the forehand and backhand swing, moving his racket slowly through the air, emphasizing the follow-through.

"Okay, now try to hit the ball back to me." Jeff motioned Macario to the other side of the net.

Jeff hit a gentle shot to Macario's forehand. With both hands on the racket, Macario swung at the ball. He missed.

The guys pointed at Macario and laughed again.

"No, no, it's not baseball," called Jeff. "Use only one hand. Don't try to kill the ball. Just lift it over the net in a nice arc."

Macario sent the next one high above Jeff's head, much to the delight of their audience. They hit a few more shots back and forth, Jeff making each return as easy as possible. When he figured it was time to end the session, he raced in on the ball, smashing it past Macario's side.

Everyone hooted and clapped.

"This is great. Thanks a lot, you guys," Jeff said. He hoped they knew he meant it. "I'd better get back." He returned the rackets and balls to Santiago.

"*Gracias*," said Santiago, extending his free hand.

"Don't thank me," said Jeff, as they shook. "*Gracias* to you."

When Jeff arrived at the field Thursday morning, he knew something was wrong.

Alexa was leaning against a stack of empty crates with her arms crossed and her head bent.

"What's the matter—still waking up?" he tried to joke. "Want a sip of Martha's cooked coffee?"

She barely shook her head.

Jeff had never seen Alexa down. Angry or disgusted, yes, but not down.

"They got our house."

"What do you mean?"

"During the night. Someone left a dead opossum on our front porch and beer bottles all over the lawn."

"Are you serious?" He set his coffee on the truckbed and stood in front of her.

She looked up, taking a shaky breath. "We've had vandalism before, but nothing this bad, like someone's out to get us. I'm—I'm just so tired of it." She shuddered and tears filled her eyes. "Harvest is stressful enough. I'm not getting enough sleep, and I'm not swimming, and Libby's driving me nuts, and . . . "

Jeff put both hands on her shoulders. "Hey, listen, it's going to be all right." He pulled her close and wrapped her in a hug.

Alexa pressed her face against his shoulder, muffling a rush of sobs. Jeff held her tighter. "It's okay," he whispered. Her breathing smoothed and they stood quietly. Jeff used his shirtsleeve to dry her face.

"I think it all has to do with Mexicans working for us," she said haltingly.

"Really?"

"Look at the grain tanks: 'Wetbacks go home.' That's pretty clear."

"What about the bullet holes and the irrigation valve?"

Alexa sniffled. "I don't know, but this morning there were tortillas and beans dumped on our lawn."

"Beans?"

"Yeah, all these cans of pinto beans opened and scattered all around." She chuckled wryly. "Max thought it was terrific."

"So why's someone mad about you hiring Mexicans?"

"Who knows. People get pretty strange about it. Even some of our neighbors protested when we put in the bunkhouse. It only sleeps eight but someone spread rumors that there'd be twenty or thirty guys here bringing in drugs and prostitutes."

"Has your dad talked to the sheriff?"

"Yeah, remember? The grain tank shooting—on my birthday?" She rolled her eyes. "Mom said she'd call about the house."

"Where's your mom—and Libby?" Jeff glanced around. Ethel was wandering down a row, checking the fruit and taking notes.

"Mom's still home, cleaning up and trying to settle Libby down. Libby's been crying. Says she wants to move to Alaska."

"We've got to figure this out, Alexa," said Jeff. He moved a boot back and forth through the dirt. "You know something?"

"What?"

"There's a pattern."

Alexa waited.

"What's today?"

"Thursday."

"Right. Mondays and Thursdays—bingo—we get hit. Someone's haunting around Sunday and Wednesday nights. Maybe there's something weird about the moon those nights."

"Well, then, the creeps shouldn't be too hard to catch. Let's do a stakeout. The sheriff would come for that."

"What if your dad says no?"

"He won't say no."

★   ★   ★

The next day Alexa reported back. "He said no."

"Are you serious?"

"He said he'd pass our 'excellent information' on to the sheriff and request some kind of surveillance Sunday night."

"I don't get it. Your dad doesn't seem interested at all in solving this."

Alexa sighed. "He's just so busy. And he said he didn't want any of us involved because we need our sleep for the long days we put in."

"There won't be any more long days if your farm is trashed."

Chapter 20

JEFF BOUNCED ON THE BALLS OF HIS FEET. "Come on, Kyle, let's finish this set."

"Just a second, I gotta switch rackets."

Geezuz, what was this guy trying to prove? Then Jeff remembered Macario's latest lecture. They'd been cleaning outhouses when he'd started in. "Think about the other person. Watch him hard and ask in your head what he does next? Put your mind into his. Be both places at the same time."

Okay, Kyle Yocam, thought Jeff, you're trying to upset me, but it's not going to work. He took a deep breath and closed his eyes. Concentrate, McKenzie. Focus. Look for a change of pace—maybe a light shot near the center court line. He'll expect an uncontrolled lob.

"Service!" Kyle shouted.

As the ball floated into the air, Jeff moved forward. Was he right? Yes! Easy serve. He raced for the shot and smashed it down the line. Kyle started across the court, then stopped. No way could he make it.

As he moved through the set, Jeff felt his body work

in a smoother rhythm than he could ever remember. Maybe it was those silly soccer exercises. He seemed to be quicker, too, racing over the court, hopping back and forth, finding just the right spot to return the ball. He won the set. And the next.

"Nice game," Kyle said, coming over to shake hands. "Guess I couldn't keep up with you."

Later in the afternoon, Jeff and Jason won their doubles competition. "Man, you're looking good," said Jason. "They inject something special in those strawberries?"

"Exactly." Jeff took a long drink of water from his squeeze bottle and wiped his mouth. "Actually, the guys there made a tennis court."

"What'd they do? Take out a cornfield?"

"No, idiot."

"So that's why you haven't been calling. Got a new partner?"

Jeff shook his head. "I've tried to teach a couple of them, but mostly I practice my serves. They help me with a few drills."

"Hey, berry boy." Aaron Halvorson approached Jeff and Jason, swinging his racket through a serve. "I've been keeping an eye on Debbie for you." He twirled the racket in his hand. "Too bad you've been so busy."

Jeff clenched his water bottle.

"Don't worry, McKenzie, I'm not that interested. Just consider me a temp." Aaron tucked his racket under his arm. "I think Deb was just afraid you were gonna whisper sweet nothings to her in Spanish. She wouldn't know what to do."

"You're sick, Halvorson."

"Speaking of the beaners," Aaron went on, "looks like you're turning into one. Your face is as brown as theirs." He cleared his throat and hurled spit to the ground.

"You heading south for the winter?"

"God, Aaron, give it a rest! What do you have against Mexicans, anyway?"

"Touchy, touchy." Aaron leaned to one side and cocked his head. "How come you're suddenly the almighty beaner defender?"

"I'm not their damn defender. But, for your information, they eat and sleep and piss like the rest of us so just get off their case."

"Oh, whine and cry." Aaron pretended to wipe a tear from his eye.

Jason socked Jeff's arm. "Let's get out of here."

Aaron backed up a few steps and turned to go. "Oh, by the way, I plan to get a crack at Sam Nelson at the Invitational. That guy deserves a good beating."

"Look who's talking," Jeff muttered, shaking his arm free.

Aaron grinned and walked off.

"What a jerk," growled Jeff.

"Hey, you wanna do something tonight?" Jason tapped the lid on his tennis balls.

"I don't think so." Jeff stuffed his racket in his bag.

"What are you up to, then? I mean, I hate to bring up a sore subject, but you are without a girlfriend these days."

"Do I have to have a girlfriend to do anything?" Jeff snapped. "Maybe I'd like to date a few different girls. Then maybe no one would freak out if I don't devote my entire life to just one."

★   ★   ★

Jeff stretched out on his bed. He was tired. A good tired. He didn't ache at all. And he'd won. Man, it was great to win. He thought of Macario. And Alexa.

He sat up and reached for a scrap of paper by the phone. With a quick breath, he punched the numbers.

"Hello." It was Libby.

"Is Alexa there?"

"Yeah, just a sec."

Jeff could hear her yelling: "Allexaaaa, it's a boy. It's a boy."

"Hello." Her voice was soft.

"Hi," he said. "It's a boy."

"Geez. Hi, Jeff."

"How are you?"

"I'm okay. What's up? How was your tournament?"

Jeff eased back on his pillow. "I lost my first set but nailed the next two."

"Nice goin'."

"Everything came together. I think farm work has weight training beaten by a long shot." Then he asked, "How'd the picking go?"

"Not even a full truck. We finished section four, but it wasn't pretty."

"Alexa, I have an idea."

"What?"

"Why don't we do our own stakeout tomorrow night?"

"Just the two of us?"

"Yeah. Listen, your dad isn't doing a thing about it, so someone has to."

"He asked the sheriff for extra patrolling."

"Yeah, right. That'll be one lousy pass by the farm."

She was quiet for a moment. "Well," she said hesitantly, "I don't know."

"Come on, Alexa, it's your farm. What do you think they'll hit next?"

"They're getting pretty brave. Maybe the shop.

We've got a ton of valuable tools out there and nothing's locked up."

"Sounds about right. You probably have a sign, too: 'Enter here for valuable tools.' Let's do it, Alexa," he pushed, "we'll nail these guys."

"Okay," she said slowly, then lowered her voice. "I'll meet you tomorrow night—inside the shop—at eleven."

Chapter
21

JEFF DROVE BEHIND THE LAST ROW of boysenberries and quickly shut off his engine. He sat back in his seat and stared at the swath of moonlight cutting across the black lake.

It'd been a rotten day. Nagging questions had dissolved his confidence. What if the vandals didn't come? What if they did come? Would they have guns? What would Mr. Hampton say? What would his own parents say? Not wanting to repeat the barbecue conversation, he'd told his mother he'd be at Jason's for the night.

"How's Debbie?" she'd asked, but he didn't have the patience to give a play-by-play of their breakup. "Don't worry, Mom, she can be alone once in awhile." Now he wondered about those words. Whenever Debbie broke up, there always seemed to be a quick replacement. Was Alexa like that, too? Somehow, he couldn't picture her with a boyfriend. He could, however, imagine her with himself, her arms soft around his neck, her face against his shoulder.

He pulled on his jacket, grabbed his video camera,

blanket, and flashlight and locked the door. The muffled sound of swing-shift sprinklers came from all directions. A frog croaked. A response followed. Then another and another. The chorus grew louder and louder, then stopped, leaving the night with an eerie silence.

Light from a mercury-vapor lamp filled the barnyard and shadowed the corners. Jeff slipped behind the barn and around the tennis court. As he approached the machinery shed, another light glared from the darkness. Great, he thought, no one will attempt anything with the entire world lit up. The glow came from a modular home set back against a bunch of trees. The bunkhouse. A faint murmur of voices mingled with strains of Spanish music.

Jeff moved cautiously to the shop door. As he twisted the knob and pushed against the door, a piercing squeak filled the air. He froze. Max barked from the Hampton's front porch. Damn! He heard someone shushing the dog and hurrying toward him.

"Hi," Alexa whispered breathlessly.

"Sorry about the door. Did I wake anyone?"

"I don't think so," she said, looking back at the house. "Let's stay outside, anyway."

They arranged Jeff's blanket on the ground next to the machinery shed. "I hope this works." Alexa covered their legs with another blanket.

"What if they don't come?" asked Jeff.

"Don't even think it."

A shuffling sound came from the barnyard. Then a sniffing and panting. Max. He wandered over, inspected the blankets, and climbed across Jeff's legs, his tail whacking against Jeff's chest.

"Go home," Alexa ordered hoarsely.

Max wiggled and licked her face. He sat down,

stretched out, and settled his head on her legs. "I guess we've got a bodyguard," she whispered.

Max was comfortable, the lights and music from the bunkhouse were off, and the wait began. Jeff became aware of another sound, coming from a long way off. He could almost feel the droning and thump-thumping.

"What's that?"

"What?" Alexa said.

"Listen—down the road."

"Oh, someone's baling hay."

"At night?"

"Uh-huh—the dew adds a little moisture to the hay. The animals like it better." She turned her face toward his. "You wouldn't want your hay dry, would you?"

Jeff felt his body acutely aware of her voice and her arm resting next to his. When she spoke, she smelled of peppermint and when she leaned closer, her hair brushed his cheek.

"Why did you want to do this?" Alexa said softly.

Jeff thought for a moment. While he'd been motivated to play the hero and stop the vandalism, he also knew she was a major reason. Lately, when driving to the farm, he anticipated her smile. They'd quickly slip into the day's rhythm, working through the calm of morning and the chaos of afternoon, trading stories and complaints at lunch. He'd occasionally watch as she deftly weighed flats, punched tickets, and chatted casually in Spanish. She could be tough, however, if someone challenged her scale, arguing for an extra half pound. So, McKenzie, why did you want to do this? He put his arm around her shoulder.

Alexa's body froze and she leaned forward.

Way to go, he thought. "Alexa, I—" he started.

"Shh!" She grabbed his arm.

Then Jeff heard the car. Coming from the grain tanks. He snatched the video recorder. "Let's get these jerks on film." He moved to the edge of the building, straining to see through the glare of the mercury-vapor light. As the car slowed in front of the house, Jeff peered through his lens and began filming. He felt Alexa's hand on his shoulder. Max bolted across the barnyard, barking furiously.

"Darn," Alexa said. "Max will scare them off for sure."

"Well, if he does," said Jeff, lowering the recorder, "he's scaring off a deputy sheriff."

"Oh, no," she groaned, slumping back against the shed.

The car continued down the road with Max attacking its wheels.

An upstairs light came on in the house. The front porch light snapped on, then the back porch light. Someone came out of the house and walked straight for the shop.

"I forgot to shut the door," said Jeff. He held Alexa's hand and they clung to the dark shadows.

Mr. Hampton marched up to the shop door and flipped on a light. He rustled around inside for a moment, then turned off the light and closed the door. He started back to the house when Max bounded past him and jumped up on Alexa.

"Who's there?" Mr. Hampton turned sharply, aiming his flashlight.

Jeff's heart pounded in his throat.

"Alexa? Jeff?" Mr. Hampton squinted. He looked funny with bare legs and slippers sticking out from his short bathrobe.

"Yeah, Dad?"

"What the heck is going on?"

★ ★ ★

They sat at the kitchen table across from Alexa's mom and dad.

"We were sure they'd come tonight," Alexa said weakly.

Mr. Hampton raised an eyebrow at the blankets heaped in a corner of the kitchen. "What was on your mind, Jeff?"

"Just wanted to stop this vandalism, Mr. Hampton." Oh, God, please don't let him explode.

Mr. Hampton clasped his hands on top of the table. Mrs. Hampton sat with her arms relaxed in the folds of her pink bathrobe. Her hair was loose around the collar.

"Do you remember what I said about stakeouts?" Mr. Hampton quizzed them.

"We need our sleep. Let the sheriff handle it," Alexa recited.

"And who drove by our house tonight?"

"The sheriff," she said.

Jeff wished he could help her.

Mr. Hampton cleared his throat. "More important, Alexa, what did we say about sneaking out at night? Is your memory that short?"

Alexa shifted in her chair. "No."

"And do you remember what happened last time?"

"Yes."

Jeff's mind whirled. Sneaking out at night? Last time? Then he remembered Alexa's hesitancy over the phone, and his persistence. *Come on, Alexa, it's your farm.* Now she was in trouble. Again.

"But, Dad," she said, "this was different."

"We'll see."

"Lexie," said Mrs. Hampton, "we're concerned for your safety."

"I know."

"What about you, Jeff?" asked Mr. Hampton. "Your folks know about this?"

"Well, uh, they think I'm at a friend's."

Mr. Hampton studied him. "You lied to your parents?"

"I didn't want them to worry." Jeff braced himself.

"I'd tan your hide, son, but that's not my department." He stood up. "Call your mom and dad. You figure out how to explain this. You might as well sleep on the sofa, it's so late." He looked from Alexa to Jeff. "No more stakeouts."

Chapter 22

THE NEXT MORNING JEFF leaned against the Hampton's bathroom sink and stared in the mirror at his bloodshot eyes. What a mess. He splashed cold water on his face and in his hair, then buried his head in a towel.

What a crummy night. The phone call home had not been good. After his explanation, his mother gave the classic "Thank you for letting us know, Jeffery," which meant: We'll discuss this later, but figure you're in trouble.

Mrs. Hampton had opened the living room sofa into a hide-a-bed. Once everyone had gone upstairs, questions assaulted his mind. Was Alexa asleep? Were those her footsteps above him? What was she thinking? Was she mad at him? What was this sneaking-out thing?

He looked into the mirror again and grimaced. He combed his hair with his fingers and slopped a gob of toothpaste in his mouth. He didn't care so much about his hair or his weary body. It was the hollow feeling in his gut that bothered him most. It was like he'd lost a game he should have won.

Mrs. Hampton was cracking eggs into a frying pan when he entered the kitchen. "Good morning, Jeff. How did you sleep?"

"Okay, thanks."

Alexa handed him a glass of orange juice. "Wake up."

"Did you get in trouble?" Libby bit into a piece of toast.

Jeff paused. "Well, yes and no."

"I'll bet Alexa did."

"It's none of your business," said Alexa, glaring.

"How come the bad guys didn't come?" Libby asked.

Jeff sighed. "Maybe they knew we knew."

"We're starting through the berry machines today," said Mr. Hampton as they passed the food around. "I've got to run up to Wilsonville for bearings and belts. And we'll be fertilizing corn and spraying beans for cucumber beetle." He looked at Mrs. Hampton. "Any chance for a fourth pick?"

She raised her eyebrows. "We'll give it a try. We'll have to bump the price again and push hard."

★ ★ ★

The bad guys had come. This time it was an outhouse in the strawberry field. Tipped over. With a smelly, watery slime streaming from the toilet, down a wall, and out a broken vent to a puddle on the ground.

"Yuck." Jeff wrinkled his nose as he and Macario righted the blue structure. They cleaned and scrubbed and refilled the toilet with water and disinfectant. As they worked, Jeff told Macario about the aborted stakeout.

Macario chuckled.

"What?"

"I was just thinking—that you are old goat."

"Thanks a lot."

"It is just to tease," Macario said quickly. Then he looked at Jeff. "You only say to friends."

When he returned to the truck, Jeff found Mrs. Hampton talking in low tones with Enrique Gómez.

"What's happening?" Jeff asked Alexa.

"Something about *en la noche*—in the night. And a pickup."

After *Señor* Gómez returned to his row, Mrs. Hampton explained. "He heard the vandals last night, but was afraid to do anything. Now he feels bad. He thinks he let us down, and he's offered to leave."

"What did you tell him, Mom?" Alexa asked.

"I told him he shouldn't worry or blame himself and that he and Carmen are welcome to sleep here until the strawberries are over."

★ ★ ★

The fourth pick. It sounded so ominous. At the cannery—are you going to get a fourth pick? At Martha's—are you going to get a fourth pick? So what was the big deal?

"It doesn't happen very often." Alexa was weighing a flat filled with dark red berries about the size of Jeff's fingertip. "Pickers usually leave us for the cherry harvest and the strawberries thin out or shrivel up. But if you can get a fourth pick, it's money you hadn't planned on."

Jeff scanned the field. A few less pickers than last week, but more local kids. Ethel had spread the word that this last pick was like an Easter egg hunt. "Just get the biggest ones," she'd instructed that morning. She'd even hidden little chocolate candies in the bushes and promised ice cream for those who came every day that week.

"Where were these guys when we needed them?" Jeff asked her at lunch. Ethel shrugged.

"Years ago," answered Mrs. Hampton, "the kids couldn't

wait to start picking. It was the socially accepted thing to do—out in the fields all day with their friends, boys and girls, teasing and flirting with each other, earning money for new clothes or radios. The farmers put posters up in the schools and around town and ran buses all over the place. They even had contests and prizes."

"What kind of contests?" Libby perked up.

"For the kids who came the most," said Mrs. Hampton, "and picked the most and improved the most. We gave a bicycle away one year, and we always had a big swimming party and barbecue at the end."

"Can't we do it again?" asked Libby.

Mrs. Hampton sighed. "I'd love to, sweetie, but the kids just aren't the same anymore. They don't know how to work hard."

"That's because of the ridiculous age restriction," said Ethel. "They've gotta be twelve years old to pick. Stupid." She whipped open her lawn chair and thumped it on the ground. "Like you can't pick a measly strawberry if you're ten or eleven."

"Ethel promised the kids a berry fight on the last day," Alexa told Jeff with a mischievous grin.

He eyed her. "Don't get any wise ideas."

"Who, me?" She handed him a flat.

"Yeah, you."

"Actually, I do have an idea." Alexa punched a smudged ticket.

"What?"

"You come swimming with me today after work."

Jeff lowered his voice. "What about your parents? Don't they want me out of here?"

"It's okay," Alexa whispered. "We talked about it this morning. They're not mad at you—just me."

"Are you in big trouble?"

"I can't take my driver's test for another month, now."

"No way."

"Hey, it's been worse."

Jeff eyed her. "A rebel, huh? And all along I thought you were so perfect. What's 'worse'?"

Alexa grimaced. "They took me off the swim team for two meets last year."

"Whoa! You're kidding! Pulled you from the team? I don't believe it."

She nodded. "I was really mad."

"What did you do? I mean, uh, if you want to tell me."

"Later."

Jeff stepped out of the bathhouse, pulling the drawstring tight on a pair of blue nylon swim trunks.

Alexa looked up from the fire ring. "Fit?"

"Sort of."

She leaned over and blew on a beginning flame. "Want some help?"

"Sure. We don't really need this, but I love a fire when I'm here." She brushed her hands together. "I'll change." A few moments later, she reappeared wearing a simple dark green racing suit.

"Where are all the knots?" Jeff asked.

"My drag suit? I'm not practicing today."

She started for the dock. "Race ya to the raft."

"Alexa, this is not wise. I'll probably drown."

"I've had rescue experience."

"Like what?"

"Like volleyballs." She broke into a run.

Jeff chased her to the end of the dock and dived into the murky waters.

Surfacing, he blinked and caught a splash across his face. "You!" he cried and splashed back. But she'd darted for the floating dock.

"Where've you been?" She stood above him as he grasped the edge.

He pulled himself onto the small wooden raft, then shook his head, spraying tiny droplets.

"You creep!" Alexa moved to push him in, but Jeff grabbed her wrists and tugged her toward him. She laughed and yanked back. As they pushed and pulled, the raft rose and fell.

"Stop," said Alexa, still laughing, "or we'll rock this thing over."

"Really? How?" He leaned over the side, peering into the water.

"Come on, I'll show you." She pulled him back into the water.

"You're dangerous!" Jeff sputtered, wiping his face.

Alexa brushed her hair back. "There's about two feet of air space under this thing," she said, treading water. "Just dive down and come back up inside."

Before Jeff could respond, Alexa had dipped over like a duck, her feet splashing the surface, and disappeared under the raft. Then her voice echoed, "Your turn."

Holding his breath, Jeff pushed his way through the water. When he broke the surface, he was surprised he hadn't banged his head on the low wooden ceiling.

"We used to tell spooky stories under here and make ghost sounds." Alexa cleared her throat and moaned, "Ooooohhhh."

"Super hideout," Jeff said.

"Actually, I get claustrophobic. It's like a dream. You know, when you can't get out of some place and someone's pulling your legs."

"Or the fish come to nibble your toes." He rubbed his foot against her leg.

Alexa's eyes widened in pretend horror.

He started to laugh. "It looks like your head's been cut off and it's floating around like some old bobber."

"Are you making fun of my head, McKenzie?"

"Me? Never," he protested and then, with a flashing impulse, he moved closer and kissed her lips.

Alexa sucked in a quick breath. "That's something I haven't done under here before."

"Yeah, right. I wonder how many guys you've lured under here: 'Let me show you where I hid as a kid.' You probably have a mark on one of these boards for each of them." Jeff turned around, examining the algae-covered barrels and wooden planks. Dripping water echoed in the silent, watery cave.

"Allexaaaa!" a voice called from the picnic grounds. "Where aarrre you?"

Alexa rolled her eyes. "Guess who?"

"I wonder."

"We better go or she'll get worried."

"Let her—it'd be good for her."

"Probably would, but—" she leaned forward and kissed him. "I'd better get a couple laps in today." She dunked down and splashed out of sight.

"What were you guys doing under the dock?"

"We'll never tell," Jeff answered. He rolled into a lazy backstroke. The sun was warm on his face, the water silky smooth against his body, and two kisses lingered on his lips.

Alexa wrapped a towel around her shoulders and moved closer to the fire ring. "Aren't you glad I built a fire?"

"Aren't you glad I helped?" Jeff said, tying a towel around his waist.

"Watch me!" shouted Libby as she jumped off the diving board into a floating inner tube.

Alexa waved.

"Okay," said Jeff, setting another chunk of wood in the flames, "tell me about your days as a juvenile delinquent."

She sighed. "All right." She waited a moment, then started in. "I was dating this guy, Corey, and one night I sneaked out of the house and met him by the grain tanks."

"You walked down there in the middle of the night?"

Alexa nodded. "He had a car and we went to this party. I knew my parents wouldn't let me go—it was a Sunday night and I had school the next day."

"How'd they find out?"

"I overslept, so I pretended I was sick. Mom got suspicious. Then, she found my muddy shoes outside and my sweatshirt in the laundry hamper—it smelled like cigarette smoke. I didn't smoke," she added quickly. "Mom and Dad were furious. I was grounded for a month and couldn't go to a couple swim meets."

"You are a regular JD, Alexa Hampton," said Jeff. "Let's call it even. No more digs about the bean field, okay?"

She nodded. "What'd your folks say about the stakeout?"

"I got the trust and lying lecture." He tapped his bare foot on top of Alexa's. "And, I'm not supposed to spend any extra time out here."

"You have to go?"

"Yeah, but one more question. "Why did Corey somebody's name come up when the grain tanks were vandalized?"

"You have to know *all* my secrets?"

"Yes."

Alexa picked up a long stick and poked the fire. "I broke up with Corey around Christmas. A few months later, I started dating Miguel Rosales. We went to Prom together. When we came out of the dance, we found horrible stuff sprayed on his car with shaving lotion."

"Like what?"

She paused. "Like 'wetback lover.'" We think it was Corey."

"So, you think he did the grain tanks?"

"It's possible."

"Are you still seeing Miguel?"

Alexa shook her head.

"Someone else?"

"No one."

A log broke apart, crumbling into the coals and a burst of sparks shot into the air.

Chapter 23

WHEN JEFF RETURNED from the cannery Wednesday afternoon, he found a note under his windshield wiper: *Please come up to the house—A.*

He drove into the barnyard and parked by the Hampton's back door. Max bounded off the porch and panted anxiously as Jeff climbed out of his car. "The stakeout dog. Been chasing anymore sheriff cars?" Jeff patted the smooth, black head.

Alexa opened the screen door. A white towel wrapped her head like a turban. "How was the cannery?"

"Fast." Jeff climbed the stairs and followed her into the kitchen. "It doesn't take long with a half-filled truck. Now everyone's asking when our last day will be."

"That's why I wrote you the note." She removed the towel and began combing her hair. "Looks like it's going to be tomorrow, and we're going to have a little celebration. Can you go into Sheridan with me for pop and ice cream?" She wiped her forehead with the towel. "Or do you need to practice?"

"Nah. I played well last Saturday, and I've practiced a little this week with Macario."

"Great. We can take Mom's pickup, and you can give me another driving lesson."

★   ★   ★

Alexa pulled into the Sheridan Safeway. She drove down one full row of cars and started back on another when Jeff tapped her shoulder.

"What?"

He pointed to a faded green pickup parked one aisle over. Danny Stevens stood by the opened passenger door while a stocky guy with a buzz cut climbed out. The guy wore a sweatshirt with its sleeves cut off and "Bob's Gym" plastered across the back. His biceps were proof enough he worked out. Another guy slammed the driver's door. He stopped for a moment, fumbling in his camouflage shirt pocket, then pulled out a cigarette and cupped his hands to light it. Danny grabbed a box of empty beer bottles from the back of the pickup and they headed for the store entrance.

"Look." Jeff pointed to the pickup. "There's a .22 across the back window."

"So?"

"Maybe it's the same .22 that shot your grain tanks full of holes."

Alexa paled. "Can you be sure?"

Jeff shrugged and dumped brass shells from an empty coffee mug. "I never threw these away. Let's check it out."

"You've gotta be kidding. What if we get caught?"

"Then we get caught."

They walked casually toward the pickup. "My hands are cold," Alexa whispered.

Jeff grasped one; it was clammy. "Keep an eye on the store. I'm just gonna look around." With a squeeze to her hand, he moved quickly to the passenger door and peered through the window. A flannel shirt lay jumbled on the seat. Empty beer cans and dusty pop cups littered the floor. He tried the door. It opened with a jerk. He heard Alexa gasp. Bending down, he examined the floor, moving cans and corn dog wrappers aside. Then he pulled open the glove compartment. Paper napkins, DMV envelopes, catsup containers, a can of chew, a key.

"Looking for something?"

Jeff's heart stopped. Oh, God, this was it. He straightened up and looked toward the voice. An older man stood beside a car parked in front of the pickup. He held a small sack of groceries in one arm and was unlocking his door with the other hand.

"Uh, yeah." Please, don't let my voice crack, begged Jeff, his mind racing. "Uh, a grocery list. From my mom. She'll kill me if I forget anything."

"Hurry up, Jeffery," urged Alexa. "We gotta get home."

"I know how that goes." The man pointed to his sack. "I'm here for my wife, but she's going to have a fit. I got more than my list." He chuckled as he opened the door. "Well, good luck."

"Thanks." Jeff smiled weakly, then, with a quick glance at Alexa, he turned back to the glove compartment. He moved aside the napkins and caught his breath. The bottom of the compartment was covered with .22 cartridges. Jeff crammed one into his pocket. He shut the glove compartment and was about to leave when something beneath the flannel shirt caught his eye. He pushed the shirt aside. A paramilitary magazine was folded to a diagram of pumps and pipes. He flipped back the page. The words "Disabling Water Systems" sprawled across the top. His throat tightened.

"Jeff," whispered Alexa hoarsely, "they're coming."

He quickly covered the magazine, shut the door, and ducked down. "Come on." He led the way around the next car. They crouched low and stared silently at each other.

Someone dropped a sack in the back of the pickup. "That oughta keep us going tonight," said a rough voice. Probably Workout Man. Both doors opened and slammed shut. The pickup started and backed out.

Jeff and Alexa inched their heads above the car and watched as the pickup rumbled away. Alexa closed her eyes and let out a breath. Jeff helped her stand up. "Are you okay?"

"I'm shaking," she said.

He put his arm around her. "Did you get a good look at them?"

"The one with the camouflage shirt was really scuzzy— he had long, brown, greasy hair in a ponytail and a beard. I didn't have time to check out the other guy."

Jeff pulled the .22 shell from his pocket. "I found this," he said, squinting to read the imprint. "R-E-M." He pulled a grain tank shell from another pocket and compared. "Same."

It wasn't until they'd gotten the pop and ice cream and were driving back to the farm that Jeff remembered the magazine. "It was one of those survivalist, soldier-of-fortune things. They had it open to an article on destroying water systems." He looked at Alexa. "Could that mean your pumps?"

"If it does, then we're in mega trouble."

"I'll bet that's it—and I'll bet it's tonight."

Chapter 24

"HAND ME THAT WRENCH, ALEXA." Mr Hampton stood inside the opening of a tall gray machine.

She slipped the wrench through a spindle covered with white plastic rods. "I know this is a sore subject, Dad, but could we talk to you about the vandalism?"

"What about it?" He grunted as he yanked on the wrench.

"We think it's going to happen again tonight."

"What makes you think so?"

"Well, it's Wednesday, and we've been hit the past two Wednesday nights."

Mr. Hampton maneuvered himself from the machine. "You think they're stupid enough to come again?"

"Probably."

"You think you know who it is?" Mr. Hampton looked like he was ready for battle, his shirtsleeves rolled above his elbows, tapping the wrench in the well of his thick hand. "Corey?"

"I don't think so."

Jeff pulled the .22 shells from both pockets. "This

one's from the grain tank shootings and this one's from a pickup in the Safeway parking lot. They both have the letters REM on the bottom." Jeff turned them up for Mr. Hampton to see.

"Lots of people use Remington shells," said Mr. Hampton.

"I know, but the kid who stole my CD player—Danny Stevens—he was in the pickup with two creepy-looking guys."

"Yeah, Dad, it's just too coincidental," Alexa argued. "And we think they might go for our pumps."

Jeff explained the trip to Sheridan, the pickup, and the magazine.

"Well, then, they've gone too far if they're after our water supply." Mr. Hampton's hands were on his hips now, reminding Jeff of that night on the McKenzie's front lawn.

With a quick twist, Mr. Hampton had his radio off his belt and up to his mouth calling Macario, Santiago, Jerónimo, and Casimiro.

Jeff tried to recognize a few words. He looked at Alexa.

"He's telling them to come to the house tonight at eleven."

★   ★   ★

The Hampton kitchen was buzzing with Spanish chatter when Jeff arrived. He sensed he was not the only anxious one in the room. The guys greeted him with rapid *"Holas"*.

"You are detective," Macario said with a smile.

"Do your parents know where you are?" Mr. Hampton looked up from the kitchen table where he was drawing something on a piece of paper.

"Yes, sir."

"Yes, sir!" Libby mimicked, saluting.

Jeff returned the salute as he stepped past the table, joining Alexa and Mrs. Hampton.

"I'd better get to go," Alexa spoke quietly in Jeff's ear. "Dad acts like I'm staying home."

"Here's the plan," announced Mr. Hampton.

Everyone crowded around. He held out a rough map. "The ladies will let us know if anyone comes to the house, or drives by." He pointed to a crude drawing of the house. "Santiago will be here behind the grain tanks to watch Bethel Road from the south." Santiago nodded. "Casimiro, you'll be just north of the bean field, in Mr. Feldman's barn. Jerónimo, let's put you in the cattails near the corn. Macario, Jeff, and I will be in the oak trees, here, near the pumps."

"But, Dad," said Alexa, "this was my idea, too. Please let me go."

"You can help from the house."

"Come on, Dad, I'm perfectly capable. I won't get in the way, honest. Please. I can sit in the cattails with Jerónimo so we can surround them."

Mr. Hampton paused for a moment, then said, "Okay, you can help Jerónimo, but you'll do as you're told out there."

"All right!" Alexa grinned at Jeff.

"That's not fair." Libby crossed her arms. "You're treating me like a baby."

"No, I'm not." Mr. Hampton stood up and kissed her forehead. "I need your help here, sweetie. They've been bold enough to come to the house once and they could do it again. I'm depending on you and Mom to keep a constant lookout. No lights or TV, remember."

"Whatever," Libby said.

"Here are blankets," said Mrs. Hampton, handing out an assortment of worn bedding.

"Don't forget," said Mr. Hampton, tapping his radio, "our voices carry in the night, so only important calls. Let us know if anyone's coming from your direction."

With repeated "*Que le vaya biens*," they filed out the back door. Santiago and Casimiro left in separate pickups. Jerónimo and Macario climbed into the back seat of Mr. Hampton's pickup.

"Nervous?" Jeff asked Alexa as they slipped in the front.

"Not tonight. I'm ready for these jerks."

Jeff could see the firm outline of her face shadowed from the porch light. When she looked at him, the determination faded to a scowl. "They'd better come tonight or we'll really look stupid."

"I thought of that." Jeff reached for her hand.

Mr. Hampton shut the driver's door and started the engine. "Let's get this over with."

They passed Santiago parking behind the grain tanks. Farther down Bethel Road, they could see Casimiro turning into the Feldman's barnyard.

Mr. Hampton drove carefully through the strawberry field, his pickup lights guiding the way down the dirt road. He moved around the ruts and stopped once to push a wheelie into a row. At the cattails, he let Alexa and Jerónimo out, warning them to be quiet and careful, then he pulled in behind the oak trees.

Jeff thought of Carmen and Enrique. They were nowhere around.

Following Mr. Hampton's cues, Jeff remained silent and scanned the darkness for any sign of activity. His eyes had grown accustomed to the night and, with faint light from the moon, he could make out the undulating berry rows, the shadowed towers of empty flats, and piles of wheelies. The Ford truck seemed to stand guard, waiting patiently at the crossroad.

"This is Santiago." The quiet voice splintered the night. "A *carro* is coming to you."

Mr. Hampton rose to his knees, adjusting binoculars to his eyes. Macario and Jeff stayed low, watching as the car moved erratically down the road, weaving back and forth, flashing light from one side to the other. Was this how he'd looked that night with Paul?

"*Mala suerte,*" whispered Macario as the car passed by the strawberry field.

"It's okay," said Mr. Hampton, sitting back against a tree. "Be patient."

"Right, Macario," said Jeff. "Patience. Remember our advice at the barbecue? Have you been practicing?"

"*Sí.* But my mouth says the words before I can remind it. My brothers, they are ready to move me to the shop."

"Shh," warned Mr. Hampton.

Jeff took in a deep breath. The sweet scent of ripe strawberries hung on the dew. He thought of Alexa and listened for the possible sound of her voice floating on the cool air. Then his eyes wandered across the open sky and settled on the half moon. Not too far from its base was a bright star. He stared at the crescent shape and the lone star. Something tugged at his mind. The moon and the star. The big and the small.

His memory clicked. The hawk and the swallow. Was the star after the moon? Did everything in the world have something nagging, harassing, pecking? Jeff closed his eyes for a moment. He thought of his parents and their endless reminders to practice, to see Debbie, to play hard. And Mark's tiresome jabs. Then he remembered Mr. Stevens yelling at Danny and grabbing his arm.

"Hey," came Macario's guarded voice, "*Despierta, andas caminando por los cielos.*"

"What?"

"I tell you wake up, you are walking through the sky. Maybe like you say daydreaming."

"I am Casimiro." The voice came suddenly from the radio.

"Yes," Mr. Hampton answered.

"Pickup is coming."

"*Gracias.*"

Again they crouched to the ground, Mr. Hampton peering through his binoculars.

Jeff strained to hear. There it was. The sound of tires crunching over gravel, but no lights. The noise stopped. Jeff could see a fuzzy blob on the road. Now it turned into the field.

"They're driving straight through the berries!" Mr. Hampton whispered.

Jeff watched as the outline grew stronger, smashing across the Bentons. He could feel his pulse throbbing in his neck. He tried to swallow, but his throat was coarse and dry. He drew in a deep breath as the pickup passed in front of the oak trees and creaked to a stop at the edge of the lake. Headlights suddenly flashed on, aiming down the bank at the pumps. Doors opened and two people climbed out from the passenger side and one from the driver's side.

"All right!" It was the driver. "We're gonna have ourselves a party."

"Is that the pickup?" Mr. Hampton asked Jeff.

"That's it."

"How about the fellows?" He handed Jeff the binoculars.

Jeff squinted as they moved in front of the headlights. "Same ones. Yeah, and there's Danny Stevens." Workout

Man carried a six-pack. Long Hair had a rifle. They all stood for a moment at the top of the embankment, then Long Hair aimed at the water. Crack! The binoculars whacked into Jeff's face. "Geezuz!" he whispered.

"Stay down," Mr. Hampton growled. "Maggie," he breathed into his radio, "don't talk, just call the sheriff."

Now Workout Man was handing out beer. Long Hair gave Danny the rifle. There was some mumbling and laughing. Then Danny turned, aimed, and fired. The shot struck metal.

The control panel!

"Freeze!" shouted Mr. Hampton. "We have you surrounded. Drop the gun and place your hands on top of your head."

"Damn!" someone shouted. Jeff could see Danny holding the rifle at his side, looking to the oak trees.

"Drop the gun," repeated Mr. Hampton.

Danny tossed it down.

"Come on!" ordered Long Hair. All three jumped for the pickup. The engine squealed and the wheels spun. With the doors still swinging open, the pickup turned around.

Macario bolted from the trees, sprinting to the escaping pickup.

"Macario!" Jeff lunged after him.

"Jeff—let's go." Mr. Hampton raced for his pickup. Jeff followed on his heels. They scrambled in and slammed the doors. Mr. Hampton started the engine and shifted in one swift move. They sped from the oaks, lights bearing down on the faded green pickup and on Macario, now bracing himself against the culprits' cab.

The fugitives clipped a stack of flats.

Mr. Hampton raced for the main road as the vandals cut through the field. Jeff held his breath as he watched the runaway pickup bounce through the ditch, swerve across the gravel road, smack into the far ditch, and go airborne. Something flew from the rear of the pickup. Jeff's heart stopped. "Macario!"

Mr. Hampton pulled onto the road and spun to a halt alongside the bean field. Jeff jumped from the cab, leaped across the ditch and stumbled. He pulled himself back up, running as he regained his balance.

"Macario. Are you all right?" He dropped to his knees, panting.

Macario rolled side to side, grasping his left shoulder with his right hand. "*Sí*," he said taking a sharp breath. "I am fine."

"No, you're not." Jeff put his hand on Macario's arm.

"Geezuz, Maco, you trying to play hero?" Mr. Hampton bent down.

"No, no. Just want to stop the *bandidos*."

The sound of sirens came faintly from a distance.

Mr. Hampton stood again. "You fellas stay in your rig," he bellowed at the pickup, which was stuck in the freshly irrigated field.

"Jeff!" Alexa tripped across the bean rows.

He stepped forward, catching her fall.

"I was so worried," she gasped.

"I'm okay. It's Macario."

"Macario! Oh, no," she choked. Kneeling, she leaned over and grasped his hand. "We'll take care of you."

Chapter 25

JEFF SCANNED THE MADRONA HILLS parking lot. Don't plan on it, he warned himself again as he turned slowly, studying the crowd milling about the groomed lawns. A cheer rose from the nearest court.

"Women's single semi-finalists, please report to the tournament desk." The announcement was punctuated with the sound of tennis balls pounding against tight rackets and warm asphalt.

Sunday on the farm, Jeff tried to convince himself, was as busy as any other day. They didn't have to come for the entire day, he argued, or even for an entire match . . . just come.

He walked over to the draw sheet and found his name posted with Ty Madsen's. Jeff tried to remember Ty. Strong backhand? Dynamite serve? Sam Nelson's name was a few brackets down, and Jeff wondered if the day would bring them together.

He wandered back to the courts and stared at the spectators. White polo shirts, hats, and sunglasses. What would the guys wear if they came? Clean jeans, probably, and clean work shirts. He'd never seen them dress up. What if they felt out of place?

Jeff sighed as he looked back to the parking lot. Even his parents and Mark hadn't shown up. Maybe they wouldn't come at all. Moving to the shade of a tree, he sat down against the trunk. Suddenly, he felt very tired. It seemed weird to be at the club. Sort of unreal, like the hospital felt the other night.

The ambulance had taken Macario to the emergency room. Jeff, Alexa, Mr. and Mrs. Hampton, Libby, and Macario's brothers had followed and managed to take up most of the waiting room. Everyone whispered, like they'd wake someone if they talked at a normal volume. They leafed through old magazines, stared at the ceiling or the floor, or closed their eyes.

Mr. and Mrs. Hampton were allowed behind closed doors. They'd come out every now and then to report: X rays, tetanus shot. Dislocated shoulder. Questions and forms. Pain medicine. Manipulations and relocated shoulder, bandages and sling. No work for six weeks.

It was so unfair. Macario laid-up for over a month and the creeps probably wouldn't see the inside of a jail. At least they'd been handcuffed and taken away in patrol cars. The rifle and .22 casings had been seized as evidence; a tow truck had been ordered for the pickup.

The sheriff called the hospital. Long Hair was Shawn Stevens, Danny's older brother, and Workout Man was Shawn's buddy. The three were interviewed separately and each confessed to the streak of vandalism. Revenge. That's what it was. Revenge for Danny's firing and something about Mexicans taking jobs at the steel mill. Why the Sunday and Wednesday night pattern? They had Mondays and Thursdays off.

The late night held one more encounter for Jeff: his parents.

They were awake when he returned home and his dad called him to their bedroom.

"How'd it go?" asked his dad, propped up on the pillow behind his back.

"Great. We nailed 'em." Jeff stood at the foot of their bed explaining the stakeout, the chase, and the hospital. He left out the gunfire part.

"You need your rest for Saturday's Invitational, Jeff," his dad said. "You didn't have to go to the hospital, you know. That's Mr. Hampton's job."

"It's not a job, Dad. We were taking care of a hurt man."

"One of the Mexicans, right?"

"One of the employees," Jeff said firmly. "And, my friend."

His mother got out of bed, padded over to Jeff, and hugged him. "You're all right—that's the most important thing."

"Uh-huh."

"I'm sure Debbie will be relieved."

"Mom, in case you haven't noticed, Debbie and I broke up."

She sat on the edge of the bed. "You didn't."

"We did. And please don't call her. It won't work this time." He turned to leave. "I've invited the Hamptons and the crew to the Invitational."

His father snatched his glasses from the nightstand. "Jeffery, what were you thinking? The Mexicans won't even know what's going on."

The veins throbbed in Jeff's neck and the words came in a rush. "The *Mexicans* built me a tennis court, Dad. I think they know *what's going on*. Besides, isn't clapping an international language?"

Mr. McKenzie removed his glasses and reached for the lamp. "I'm going to sleep. We've got a tournament tomorrow."

"Wait a minute, Dad. *I've* got a tournament tomorrow. If you want to come, fine, but don't be rude."

"Jeffery, have you ever seen me rude?"

"We'll be very friendly," assured his mom.

The match with Ty Madsen was not pretty, but Jeff managed a win. Now it was late afternoon and a knot claimed his stomach. Standing by an outdoor drinking fountain, he dropped two Alka-Seltzer tablets in a cup of water.

"What's the matter, buddy? Nervous tension build up?"

Jeff knew the voice and the knot twisted. Aaron Halvorson held a Nike tennis bag in one hand and Debbie's hand in the other.

"Hi, Jeff." Debbie adjusted her sunglasses.

"I washed out," said Aaron. "Looks like you get Sam Nelson again after all."

"Looks like it," said Jeff.

"Where's your rally squad?" Aaron glanced around. "I expected half of Mexico to show up."

"Here's his rally squad." Jason joined them and slugged Jeff's shoulder. "Why don't you get lost, Halvorson?"

"Don't tell me there are two beaner lovers at Madrona Hills, now. I suppose next you'll be promoting half-priced memberships for wetbacks."

"Come on Aaron, let's go." Debbie tugged at his arm.

It was hardly Centre Court at Wimbledon, but it was center court. He'd made it to the championship match, even though it had taken every ounce of concentration. Each game so far had been a battle of the brain. He'd be ready to serve and he'd think of Alexa. Or he'd race across court and he'd be chasing Danny.

As Jeff took his racket out of his bag, he heard a commotion in the bleachers. Mrs. Hampton and Ethel were climbing up to an empty row. Alexa, Libby, Mr. Hampton, Macario, and all the guys waited on the ground. Everyone wore jeans or slacks and a navy blue T-shirt with something written on one side. Everyone, that is, except Libby, who was head-to-toe in white. Macario wore his White Sox hat. And his sling.

"Hey, Jeff!" Libby waved.

"Howdy," he said, walking over to the group. His stomach relaxed. "Thanks for coming. This is great." He examined the T-shirts. "Hampton Farms" the lettering read in an arc over a clump of red strawberries and green leaves. "Pretty nice."

"Dad got these yesterday to surprise us," Alexa said. Her blond hair glowed against the dark shirt.

"Greetings," came a voice behind Jeff. He tensed. His father placed a hand on Jeff's shoulder. "Good luck."

"Thanks." Jeff took a deep breath. Don't embarrass me, he thought.

"Go for it," said Mark, giving Jeff a thumbs-up.

Mr. Hampton shook Mr. and Mrs. McKenzie's hands.

"Jeff's debt is paid off now," Mr. Hampton told them, "but I sure could use him the rest of summer. He's a good worker," he glanced at Macario, "and I'm one short for a while. The job's yours, Jeff, if you want it."

He didn't know what to say. He'd paid off the irrigation motor. He could return to the club and his tennis, locker room parties, the whole bit.

"That's nice of you to offer, Mr. Hampton," Mrs. McKenzie was saying, "but I'm sure Jeff's anxious to get back on the courts."

Jeff looked at the group of solemn faces. These guys might not know much English, but they sure as heck knew what was going on. He broke the stillness with a round of introductions, which started a chorus of hellos and nods and polite smiles. The McKenzies didn't shake hands, but they were civil.

"Hey, all right, the rally squad made it." Aaron walked by and elbowed Jeff. Debbie followed, eyeing the Hamptons. "Kick butt, McKenzie," said Aaron as he and Debbie sat in the front row.

Every nerve in Jeff's body bristled as he walked to his bench. He put a leg up and bent over, stretching, breathing slowly, trying to refocus. He stretched the other leg, jumped in place a few times, and swung each arm in large circles.

Sam was at his bench now, drinking from a water jug. He wiped his hands and face on a towel and looked over at Jeff. "I haven't seen you since last year. How's it going?"

"Okay." They both moved to the net and shook hands.

"I thought you'd be at Hillsboro or Corvallis," said Jeff.

"I haven't played much tennis this summer. I've been traveling a lot—checking out colleges for next year."

"Looking for a tennis scholarship?"

"Me?" Sam spun his racket in his hand. "Nah. This is as far as I go. I'm looking at an engineering major. I'll be lucky to go to the bathroom, let alone have time for tennis tournaments."

The umpire and linesmen entered the court.

"Well, good luck," said Jeff.

"Thanks. Same to you."

Jeff returned to his bench. He pulled his socks up and tightened his shoelaces. He wiped his hands on a terry cloth towel. Then he opened a new, pressurized can of tennis balls, listening to the familiar hiss, breathing in the rubbery, pungent smell. His adrenaline jumped into high gear. He wanted to win this match, yes, but mostly he wanted to play well. He gripped his racket and walked onto the court.

Warming up, Jeff and Sam hit ground strokes and served for a few minutes. Then the umpire signaled them to the sidelines where he flipped a coin. Jeff called heads. It was tails and Sam chose to serve. The crowd quieted, and the umpire climbed into his chair.

Jeff moved to his baseline. He glanced at the bleachers. Alexa sat up straight and shaded her eyes. Libby waved. Jeff raised his racket, then faced the net. He watched Sam move into position. Jeff hopped on the balls of his feet.

"Are the players ready?" asked the umpire.

Sam and Jeff nodded.

"Let's play."

Jeff braced for the serve. Whack! The ball screamed to the corner of the service box. He lunged and swung his racket, making perfect contact. The ball exploded off the strings and dipped sharply after it crossed the net.

Back it came. Jeff raced for the baseline shot, ready with a tight backhand. The instant he felt the hit, he ran for the net, secured his position, and smashed the next shot crosscourt. Sam never had a chance to retrieve it.

"Love-fifteen," announced the umpire.

A loud whoop went up from the Hampton crew.

"Nice play," Sam called.

They moved through the first set with Jeff winning six games to Sam's three.

"You've got him where you want him," Jason called as Jeff took a drink of water. Aaron sat with his arms crossed and Debbie took off her sunglasses, tipped her head slightly, and offered Jeff a sweet smile. Oh, geez, thought Jeff. What did she want now?

The next set was different. Jeff could feel Sam shedding his pleasant mood and turning serious. The balls pounded back and forth. Sam picked up the pace, tearing to the net, and smashing his returns. Jeff felt dazed. What happened to Mister Easy Going?

He struggled to keep up. He knew he'd lost his focus. Someone coughed and he cringed. A plane flew overhead and he clenched his racket. He looked at Alexa. She bit her lip. Macario was expressionless. Maybe they shouldn't have come.

Trailing now one game to Sam's three, Jeff doublefaulted and turned over the serve. He took several deep breaths and danced around on his feet. He swung his racket through the air. Come on, McKenzie, get a grip.

Sam took the set, six-four.

Jeff sat down and gulped more water. He could see Alexa out of the corner of his eye talking to Macario. What would she do if she was behind in a swim meet?

He draped a towel over his head, blocking out the rest of the world. He thought of Sam. Who is this guy going off to college to study engineering? He's giving up tennis. Yeah, but he wants to go out a winner. Think about it, McKenzie. He's been hitting strong serves and attacking the net. He's also moving around his backhand. So deal with it, stupid.

He stood up and walked over to his baseline.

Sam addressed the court. "Service." Jeff studied the ball, then expanded his focus to the full court, trying to feel the toss, the swing, the direction of the hit. There it was. Jeff stepped into the shot and sent the ball to Sam's feet. Sam shoveled it back and charged the net.

Okay, McKenzie, over his head, Jeff coached himself as he lobbed the ball. It kissed the baseline. Yes! He felt a surge of energy. Keep it up, buddy. Now let's attack his backhand.

As they moved through the next few points, Jeff hammered at Sam's backhand, hitting shots deep to the corner. Sam's feet couldn't maneuver fast enough. At the same time, Jeff realized his own footwork was quick and snappy, changing directions, moving backward or forward or scooting sideways.

You're on a roll, Jeff told himself, exhilarated. Yes. Just keep it going and you've got the trophy.

With a piercing cross-court net shot, he took the first game. The Hampton crew shouted and clapped. Macario and Jerónimo were standing. Jeff smiled. Every bone in his body felt proud.

After winning the second game, Jeff went to his bench. He wiped his face. His eyes ached from squinting into the late afternoon sun. Drinking from his water jug, he heard Aaron's voice, "Looks like you've won the beaners' hearts. Better win for them, Jeff. You don't want to disappoint 'em. They may go back to Meh-hee-co."

Heat flushed Jeff's face. Slowly he set his jug down. He turned and glared at Aaron. Aaron's expression shouted, "You can't touch me here." Jeff's eyes narrowed and he clenched his jaw. He stood up and walked toward Aaron.

"Let's play tennis," called the umpire.

Aaron's face now challenged, "I dare you."

The crowd hushed as Jeff came closer. "These are my friends, Halvorson, so keep your big mouth shut. I'm sick and tired of your stupid comments. Grow up."

"Hey, man, you've got some nerve bringing them here," Aaron pushed.

Jeff lunged at Aaron, grabbing his shirt. "And you're a racist pig, Halvorson."

"Warning to Mr. McKenzie for delay of game," said the umpire firmly.

"I don't know what's eating you," fired Jeff, ignoring the order, "but keep it to yourself. The rest of us don't want to hear it."

"Time violation," the umpire announced into the microphone. "Penalty point goes to Mr. Nelson. I urge you to take your place, Mr. McKenzie."

Jeff's eyes shot up and met Macario's. Macario pointed to his head and moved his lips: "Think." Jeff hesitated, then took a deep breath and shoved Aaron back in his seat. He turned on his heels and walked away without looking back. His eyes twitched and his arms shook. With another drink, he slobbered water down his chin.

A linesman tapped him on the shoulder. Jeff grimaced. Now what? He jerked around. The linesman held out a baseball cap. The words said "White Sox." Jeff looked back at the stands. Macario's black hair glistened in the sun. Jeff swallowed hard, then waved the hat and placed it on his head.

Now concentrate, Jeff told himself as he changed courts. "Love-fifteen," he called. His left arm rose, his hand opened, and the ball soared into the air as his right arm swung back, arched, and smashed though.

The ball thundered low across the net. Ace! Yes! In your face, Aaron, he thought.

Everyone clapped. Not just the Hamptons and his parents. Everyone.

Then it happened. That rare, sweet occasion when everything comes together. The ball suddenly seemed bigger and slower and easier to see. Jeff felt his body turn light and graceful as he reacted without thinking. He was in tune with every movement on the court. He was in the zone.

With one last volley, he charged the net, held his racket up, and met the ball. Sam missed the final shot. That was game, set, and match.

"Bravo!" Jeff could hear his dad.

"¡Bravísimo!"

The entire Hampton gang was on its feet, clapping and shouting. Macario held a proud smile. Jeff's eyes moved down to the first row. Aaron was gone but Debbie was still there. Her look said *come see me*.

Chapter 26

"NICE GAME." Sam approached the net and offered his hand.

"Thanks." Jeff shook it. "Good luck at college."

Jeff's eyes were suddenly covered with two soft hands. "Congratulations," whispered Debbie. She kissed his ear.

Jeff pulled away. Now someone pounded his shoulder. "Awesome game." Mark jumped in front of him.

"All right! Way to go!" Jeff's dad grasped his arm and shook his hand.

"Wonderful game," said Mrs. McKenzie. She hugged him. "I'm so proud of you, darling." Then she spotted Debbie. "Oh, it's so good to see you."

Debbie smiled and hung close to Jeff as the Hamptons and the guys congregated at the base of the bleachers. Jeff looked for Alexa. She stood near the rear of the group beside Macario. Jeff quickly threaded his way to her. "You okay?"

"I wasn't sure about you and Debbie."

"I'm sure."

He pulled her back through the group to the center. "Stay here, next to me, okay?" He entwined his fingers with hers.

Alexa nodded.

"Jeff." Debbie flipped her sunglasses to the top of her head. "Are you going to the barbecue and dance?"

"I don't think so."

"They'll be giving out the awards at the dance. Don't you want to get that big, gorgeous trophy?"

"My folks will pick it up."

"Fine," snapped Debbie. She swung around and pushed through the crowd.

Mrs. Hampton held up a Hampton Farm T-shirt. "This one's for you. Congratulations, Jeff."

"Hey, thanks a lot."

"And we have an extra ticket to the St. Paul Rodeo," said Alexa.

"All right."

"You can sit next to me," said Libby.

Jeff gave her a high five.

The group drifted toward the exit. "I'll catch up to you," Jeff told Alexa. He dodged between people, hurrying to Macario's side. "Thanks, Maco, for all your help."

Macario shook his head. "You would have done a good job."

"No way. If it weren't for you, I'd have lost it off the court."

"The *güero*?"

"Yeah, wasn't he a jerk?"

"*Sí. Muy feo.*"

Jeff laughed. "*Gracias, muchas gracias,*" he told the rest of the guys. They reached to shake his hand and pat his back. He looked again at Macario and felt a sudden tightening in his throat. Macario's eyes were moist. Jeff took off the White Sox cap and handed it to him.

"No, it is for you. Maybe bring you good luck." Macario grinned.

"It already did." Jeff put it back on his head. "Thanks."

Returning to his bench, Jeff gathered his racket and bag and water. He looked around the empty tennis courts and mentally replayed his best shots. Sweet, he thought. How very sweet.

The early evening air was still hot and the tangy smell of barbecued chicken mingled with the scent of freshly cut grass. People were chatting in small groups or lazily strolling along pathways.

Macario and several of the guys stood in a circle on the lawn. Macario waved for Jeff to join them.

As Jeff got closer, he could see a waiter at the center of attention.

"This is *mi primo*," Macario said, "my cousin, Sergio González."

Jeff gripped Sergio's extended hand, shaking it once and then a second time.

"*Mucho gusto*," said Sergio.

"*El gusto es mío*," returned Jeff.

"Ah, *mucho español*."

"No," Jeff denied.

"*¿Como se llama?*"

"Jeff."

"*His nombre*," interrupted Macario, "is *Don* Jeff."

"You calling me names?" Jeff knew the honor of the title and he suddenly felt awkward.

Macario rescued him. "Sergio has letter yesterday from his *esposa* and there is much rain. The garbanzos and corn will be okay this year."

"Good deal," said Jeff.

"Come on you guys," Libby called. "The rodeo's going to start in half an hour."

Jeff met up with Alexa at the edge of the parking lot. "Any chance your dad will let me take you to the rodeo?"

"I heard that," came Mr. Hampton's voice behind Jeff. "What is our policy, Maggie, regarding employee dating?"

"I don't think there is a policy," said Mrs. Hampton.

"Do we need one?"

"Do we have an employee?"

"I guess that's up to Jeff."

Alexa was trying to appear nonchalant, but her mouth twisted into a smile.

Jeff turned around. "Same time as always?"

"Yup. Macario will explain to you the fine art of training blackberry canes."

"Oh, Dad," protested Alexa, "not that."

"Would you like to help?"

"No, I mean, well, yes, but . . . "

"Jeff will do just fine. And you, Alexa, will start mowing the strawberries down."

"Awesome."

Jeff opened the passenger door for Alexa. "Wait," he said, holding her arm. He leaned back against the car and drew her close. "Thanks for coming today."

"I was nervous for you."

"Me, too."

"I'm surprised you're coming back to the farm." She looked at him curiously. "What about tennis?"

"Did you forget?" Jeff asked, "I have my own, private court. Besides, I've got to carve my name underneath a raft."

Alexa smiled. Jeff held her for another moment as his eyes moved slowly across the manicured landscape, the empty tennis courts, and the clubhouse. He looked at the sky—the same sky that stretched over a farm near Sheridan, Oregon. The same sky that looked over an oak knoll, an irrigation pond, a strawberry field . . . and a bean field. And, far, far to the south, over a garbanzo field.